I0529619

Denizens of Distant Realms

Dawn Vogel

Cover Art by Leigh Legler

CONTENTS

THE COBBLER'S DAUGHTER

———

When Chetana's father died, her uncles would not allow her to see the body. Their insistence made no sense. This was not the first time a member of the family had died. Chetana was only a toddler when her grandmother died, and yet she had helped to wash the body. Her brother had died two years previous, and she had accompanied his body to the funeral pyre, as was traditional.

Uncle Lochan said, "It is time for you to take on more responsibility in the workshop. We have many orders to fill this week, and if we all go to the funeral, how will they get done?" He handed her a stack of shoe leathers, designs already punched through the thin paper affixed to the leather.

Chetana sat down and began to sew. When the rest of the family left for the funeral, she watched them from the window of the shop, her pile of work left unfinished. She longed to follow them, but instead shed her tears for the loss of her father in his workshop, curled up on the bench where he shaped the shoes.

On Uncle Lochan's return, he was furious. "You have done nothing?" He shook his head. "You will never fill your father's mojari." As if to make his point, he took Chetana's father's shoes and perched them on the doorframe, a silent reminder.

Three months later, they received word that the young princess had outgrown her shoes, and the queen called upon all the cobblers in the kingdom to make her daughter a new pair.

"Might I make the princess's new mojari?" Chetana asked her uncle. Her mind was already awhirl with leather dyed midnight blue and thousands of tiny gems surrounding an embroidered crescent moon.

Uncle Lochan laughed. "No, but if you are very good, I'll let you take them to the palace to present them to the princess."

The day for the journey to the palace arrived, and Uncle Lochan said nothing. He had completed the mojari for the young princess. Chetana thought they were the ugliest pair of shoes she had ever seen, even worse than her own, which were developing holes where her feet stretched them out.

"Am I to take those shoes to the princess?" she asked.

Her uncle regarded her for a long while. "No, I do not think you shall. Your attitude is poor, and once you see the splendors of the palace, I fear you would not be content here with your family. I will go myself."

Chetana watched him go. Tears threatened to spill from her eyes, but she held them back and turned them into a fiery ball of anger in her chest. As soon as Uncle Lochan was out of sight, Chetana climbed atop her father's workbench, sitting just beside the door, and pulled his shoes down from the doorframe. They were much larger than her own shoes, but they would at least give her feet room to breathe. She didn't care if her uncle saw her wearing them. She slipped her feet into the soft worn leather.

In an instant, she was content. Though she could only shuffle about in the large shoes, they still made her believe she was taller and stronger and able to stand up to her uncle.

"Now listen here—" she began. Her hand flew to her throat. The voice that had come out of her had sounded nothing like her own.

Chetana shuffled to the full-length mirror in the workshop and gasped. She recognized her own eyes, and her clothing, but her face was different. Her chin had gone from pointy and narrow to a wide square shape. *The shape of Father's jaw.* But it was not that she had taken on her father's appearance. Instead, she looked like a boy.

She grimaced and lifted her kameez so she could peek inside of her shalwar. It was not just that she looked like a boy, she discovered. Somehow, she had become a boy.

Chetana kicked her father's shoes off, still standing before the mirror. Immediately, her appearance changed back to her own.

Her head swam. It was the shoes, there was no doubt about that. But did that mean her father had only masqueraded as a man? Surely his brothers would know if he had been born a girl, but they had never said a word of the sort. And then Chetana realized why her uncles had not allowed her to see her dead father.

The gemstones on the curled toes of the mojari gleamed in the lights of the shop. Chetana was drawn to them, so much more comfortable than her own shoes. How her life would be different if she were not the cobbler's daughter, but his son. She wondered if that was why Uncle Lochan had made such a point about putting the shoes up and out of reach.

Chetana picked up her father's mojari and put them back on the door frame. Then she began digging through the piles of leather in the workshop for a similar shade.

~

By the time a year had passed, Chetana had learned much about the business of cobbling. Her uncle still had her work only on the decorative elements of the mojari he sold, but she had been working on making a pair of shoes in secret. They looked nearly identical to her father's mojari—she had even taken the time to wear them in the rain and dust to make sure they were worn out in the right places. Her feet were growing, and now were almost the same size as her father's feet had been. With just a bit of straw in the toes, she could wear the new shoes comfortably.

Chetana's feet were not the only growing feet. Again word came from the palace that the princess had outgrown her shoes. And again, Chetana asked Uncle Lochan if she might make the princess a pair of mojari. This year, her idea was inspired by a trip the family had taken to the seashore—the shoes would be simple natural colored leather, like the sand, but their adornment would be the gorgeous blues and greens of the sea. She had even brought back a handful of small shells she could use to decorate the shoes, having drilled delicate holes into each one with a blunted sewing needle.

"You are not a cobbler, Chetana," Uncle Lochan said. "You are a cobbler's daughter. I will allow you to choose what design you sew on the princess's shoes, but I will make them. And if you are well behaved, perhaps you can come along with me to deliver the shoes to the palace."

Chetana agreed, and planned to use the design she had in mind. But the mojari her uncle made were a dark and muddy green, and looked atrocious with the designs and colors she had chosen. She rubbed the outside of the shoes with sand, trying to change the color to be more like the sea, but the sand only served to make the

3

mojari dirty. She chose an elaborate design to cover up as much of the dirty green as she could, and stayed up late into the night, neglecting work on her own shoes so she could finish the princess's shoes instead.

When they were complete, Uncle Lochan took half an hour examining the shoes. His fat fingers probed Chetana's tiny stitches, trying to unravel them. But try as he might, he could not. Finally, he nodded. "Very well. You have behaved admirably, and I have no desire to make the journey to the palace this year. You may take these to present to the princess."

Chetana smiled and thanked her uncle. But making the journey on her own would be dangerous—a young woman should not travel the roads of the kingdom without an escort. She looked at her father's mojari, still perched on the door frame, where they remained except for late at night, when she needed to make sure she had rendered a part of their design correctly.

She did not go to sleep that night, as she had additions to the pair of shoes she had made as a replacement for her father's shoes. When the night was darkest, she slipped through the workshop with her handcrafted shoes. Uncle Lochan snored in his chair near the hearth, an empty jug of sura on its side nearby.

Chetana was not yet tall enough to reach the top of the door frame without assistance. Uncle Lochan's feet rested on the stepstool she normally used. Her best option was to move her father's workbench, now put away on the other side of the workshop.

The bench was too heavy for her to lift alone. When it needed to be moved during the course of the workday, she and Uncle Lochan moved it together. She could drag it across the floor if he were not around, but the noise would wake even those sleeping deeper in the house.

She spied a wooden box that held shoe leathers. If she turned it on end, it would be almost as tall as the workbench, and she could stand on tiptoe to reach the mojari above the door. She emptied the box of its contents and placed it beneath the shoes.

Chetana tested the strength of the box with one foot at first, and then added her full weight to the box. It creaked ominously, but held her. Uncle Lochan's snores continued. She released a slow breath before stretching toward the shoes. Their supple leather lay just out of reach of her fingertips. She stretched again, with more force than the previous attempt. The box teetered beneath her, and she lost her grip on her handmade shoes. She grabbed the door frame with one hand just as the box clattered to the workshop floor.

Uncle Lochan snorted and stirred. Chetana could drop to the floor and hope she landed quietly on the toppled box, or continue to hang from the door frame. She chose the latter, watching her uncle over her shoulder, eyes wide with fear.

Chetana's arm burned with the strain of holding herself up. It seemed like an eternity before her uncle turned his head away from the doorway and resumed his snoring. Chetana grabbed her father's shoes with her free hand and let go of the door frame, spreading her legs wide so she landed straddling the box she had used as a stepstool.

She sighed as she landed soundlessly. Setting her father's shoes to the side, she reset the box and prepared to put her replacement shoes atop the door frame.

~

Wearing her father's mojari, the long walk from home to the palace seemed less arduous. She had left before the sun came up, slipping out of the house before Uncle Lochan noticed her shoes or her sudden transformation into a boy. She had borrowed her father's best suit of clothing, as her own hardly fit her when she wore the magical mojari. Chetana looked, for all the world, like a young man on a very important errand.

As she walked, she couldn't help but marvel at how her father had lived his entire life in disguise. Had no one noticed he always wore his shoes, even indoors? Suddenly, Chetana felt faint. Surely it would not be permissible for her to wear her shoes into the palace.

She nearly turned back then and there. The only thing that kept her moving toward the palace was the certainty that Uncle Lochan would be furious with her if she did not deliver the shoes he had made to the princess.

Her first sight of the palace took Chetana's mind off the embarrassment that surely awaited her when she arrived. The gleaming white walls shone in the noonday sun, larger and more beautiful than any building in the town where she was born. Above the low outer wall, trees and tall flowering bushes splashed a riot of color in stark contrast to the clean white lines of the palace.

Chetana took a deep breath as she approached the guards at the gate to the palace. "I come with shoes for the princess," she murmured.

One of the guards nodded. "She is receiving cobblers in the Western Garden."

Chetana's heart leapt. In the garden, no one would insist upon her taking her shoes off. Her secret would remain safe. She thanked the guard and nearly ran to the garden on the western side of the palace.

The Western Garden was abuzz with activity. Dozens of cobblers, some of whom had brought retinues, waited in a long line that snaked amongst the ornamental architecture and paths between a variety of flowers unlike anything Chetana had ever seen.

A young man with a scroll and quill approached her and looked her over. Chetana held the shoes forward, and the young man snorted. "Who made these shoes?"

"Ah, uh—" Chetana stammered. Her father had never named his shop. It was the only one in their town, so there had been no need. She used the first thing she could think of. "The Household of Sashi."

The young man's eyes widened. "Sashi? We thought he had died."

"He did. His brother, and, uh, myself, have carried on his work."

"Hmm, brother and son, very well then." He leaned close to Chetana's ear and whispered as he gestured to the other cobblers nearby. "You're going to have to work harder if you want the princess to choose your shoes."

Chetana took a moment to look at what the other shoemakers had brought, and her heart sank. Uncle Lochan had made shoes fit for someone who lived in their town, not a princess. Around her were shoes with delicately cut leather, made to resemble a butterfly perched on the back of a pair of gold embroidered mojari. Another pair had iridescent peacock feathers layered atop one another to give the shoes they adorned wings.

She shook her head. Even her own idea would have looked shabby in comparison. As she began to turn away from the throng, settled on returning home, the young man tapped her on the shoulder.

"What's your name?" he hissed.

"Uh, Chetan," Chetana mumbled. She grimaced as soon as it had escaped her lips. Though there were boys called Chetan, it wasn't very good as an alternate name. Anyone from her town who heard about it would know right away that she was simply Chetana in disguise.

But the young man wasn't from her town. And as the princess and her mother approached Chetana, the young man called out, "May I present to you Chetan, of the Household of Sashi."

The assembled cobblers murmured and craned their necks to try to get a glimpse of Chetan. But Chetana barely noticed. Her gaze was fixed on the princess.

Chetana had always been long of limb and face. The princess had a perfectly round face, and the plump body of a girl who had never worked. But she carried herself in such a way that she was radiant. The yellow silk of her sari complimented her soft brown skin and jet-black hair that twined across her shoulder in an elaborate braid.

The princess's gaze settled on the shoes Chetana held awkwardly in front of her. She pursed her lips, and then looked up into Chetana's eyes. And then the princess smiled.

If the princess had been radiant before, now she outshone the sun itself. It took all of Chetana's willpower to not fall to her knees, weeping at the beauty of the princess.

Only the princess's soft voice brought Chetana's mind back to reality. "Thank you, but I believe they are too large." The princess arched one delicate foot toward Chetana. "Perhaps next year."

Perhaps next year. Those three words echoed in Chetana's mind for the entire journey back home. Already she was concocting a plan. She had made one pair of shoes while her uncle slept. Another pair, even mojari truly fit for a princess, was within the reach of her talents. *Next year*, she thought.

~

In the years that followed, Chetana worked tirelessly through the day, helping Uncle Lochan run the shoe shop. And then she worked on through the night to make a pair of mojari for the princess. Each year, the queen announced the princess had outgrown her shoes, and each year, Chetana donned her father's mojari to take the shoes she had made to the princess. Uncle Lochan always sent a pair of shoes with her as well, but those she tucked into the bottom of her bag.

Each year, the princess favored Chetan with a smile, but she never selected the shoes Chetana had made.

In the year the princess and Chetana were both to have their seventeenth birthday, rumors came to the village that the princess was in search of not only shoes, but also a suitor. They said she would choose her future husband from among the cobblers who brought mojari to the palace.

Uncle Lochan scoffed. "Why would the princess marry a common cobbler?" But Chetana watched him select the leather for the princess's shoes even more carefully this year. And when he brought them to Chetana to embroider, he watched over her like a hawk, making sure every stitch was perfect.

Chetana took months to decide what shoes she would make for the princess that year. She also thought for all that time about what might happen if the princess chose the shoes she made. Surely, if that happened, Chetana would be asked to come inside the palace, and would have to take off her shoes. And then the truth of her gender would be revealed.

She considered not making a pair of shoes to enter into the competition. She could take Uncle Lochan's shoes to the palace, and if the princess chose them, then Chetana could direct the girl to her uncle. But the thought of the beautiful princess marrying her uncle, who had already buried two wives, seemed abhorrent. Perhaps she should make the shoes, even if she could not marry the princess.

The thought of marrying the princess caused a sudden warm stirring in Chetana's belly. At first, she did not know what to make of it. But then she noticed the feeling came whenever a young woman who looked like the princess walked past, or came into the shop. Though it was not the same as when she thought about the princess herself, she began to realize that her feelings were adoration for the princess's beauty. She wondered if that might be something like love.

Chetana settled on a simple design for the princess's shoes, yellow leather the color of the dress that had so flattered the princess's skin, with a pattern of interlocking hearts in a simple embroidery pattern. Though they did not have the flash that many of the mojari made for the princess had, they were elegant and lovely. *Just like her*, Chetana thought.

Getting the embroidery just right was difficult. Chetana stayed up many long nights, working on the shoes and thinking of the princess.

One morning, she was awakened with a rough shake of her shoulder. Uncle Lochan glared at her from beneath dark eyebrows.

"What are those shoes for?" he asked.

Chetana had fallen asleep in the workshop, on her father's bench. The princess's mojari were in front of her, in plain sight. She tried to snatch them up, but her uncle grabbed her arms and repeated his question.

"I made them for the princess," she cried.

"For the princess? Why? She is searching for a suitor."

Chetana looked up at her uncle. His gaze flickered toward the shoes Chetana had put atop the doorframe, in place of her father's actual mojari. Then he looked back at her, and the two of them stared at one another for a long time.

Finally, Uncle Lochan spoke. "You are not a cobbler. You are only a cobbler's daughter. No princess will wear shoes you have made, let alone want to marry you. I will journey to the palace this year. You will stay here." He picked up the shoes Chetana had slaved over and threw them into the smoldering hearth.

Chetana wailed and rushed to the fireplace. The smell of singed leather reached her nostrils. She thrust her hands into the embers, barely feeling their heat. The beautiful yellow shoes were now gray with soot, blackened in places where the embers had already scorched them. "Why, Uncle? Why must you be so cruel?"

"The world is cruel, Chetana. Get used to it."

~

As soon as Uncle Lochan left the next morning, Chetana emerged from her bedroom. She had made the best of the damage instead of sleeping. Where the shoes had been scorched, she had cut out the leather, shaping the holes into hearts that matched those embroidered. Then she added more heart-shaped holes to make the mojari look like they had been fashioned that way originally. All that remained was to clean the last traces of soot from the leather, and to get to the palace by nightfall, without Uncle Lochan seeing her there.

Chetana paused in front of the mirror, her father's mojari on her feet. She looked every bit a young man, except her hair was far too long to be fashionable for a young man. She stepped out of the shoes and ran her hands through her long, straight hair. It had not been cut since her father had died.

Tears rolled down her face as she sharpened her scissors. It took a long time to saw through the first handful of hair. The dark brown strands spilled across the workshop floor, but Chetana did not bother to sweep them up. She would not be returning from the palace. She would offer her services to the princess, and if the princess did not want a royal cobbler, then Chetana would continue onward and find a village in need of someone to make them shoes.

It was nearing noonday when Chetana began her journey to the palace. She hurried as fast as she could, clutching the princess's mojari to her chest. The clouds were tinged pink and orange by the time she reached the palace.

The same young man with quill and scroll who had introduced Chetan to the assembled cobblers and palace residents the first time Chetana had come to the palace was on duty. He seemed to recognize Chetan but only frowned.

"Am I too late?" Chetan asked.

"No, but there is already a representative of the Household of Sashi who has presented his shoes to the princess."

"Can I not present mine as well?"

The scribe frowned. "In the past, the princess has seen only one pair of mojari from each shop. Wait here, please."

Chetana's fingers worried over the largest of the heart-shaped holes in the shoes while the scribe was away. Lost in contemplation, she hardly noticed when someone sat down beside her on the bench.

"Are those for me?" a soft voice asked.

Chetana looked up and found herself face to face with the princess. None of the princess's retinue was anywhere to be seen. Trying to hide her shock, Chetana said, "Yes, of course, but the scribe ... my uncle—"

The princess tilted her head to the side, a small frown creasing her brow. "May I try them on?"

Chetana nodded, pushing the shoes across the bench toward the princess.

The princess smiled and removed her old mojari. She slipped her delicate feet into the pair Chetana had made. A satisfied smile replaced her frown. The princess's gaze met Chetana's.

"I would know your name."

"I am—" Chetana began. Then she shook her head. She could not lie to the princess. She rose from the bench and stepped out of her father's mojari. "I am but a cobbler's daughter. I am Chetana, daughter of Sashi."

The princess gasped. She looked at Chetana's face, then at the shoes, and then back at Chetana's face again. "You're ... Sashi ... oh dear," she stammered.

"No, no," Chetana said. "I'm not Sashi. Sashi was my father. Or perhaps my mother. The shoes ... there's magic in those shoes. I'm sorry if I deceived you. I just wanted to make shoes you would like."

The princess smiled as Chetana spoke, and finally quieted the cobbler's daughter with a single finger placed on her lips. "You didn't deceive me. I knew all along. The shoes you make are far more delicate and beautiful than anything made by men." She paused, a blush creeping over her features. "I would like for you to make my shoes for me."

"But what about a suitor?" Chetana asked. "Won't you still need one of those?"

"I don't particularly want one. Not yet, anyway." The princess smiled shyly. "Perhaps someday, when we have gotten to know each other, you could be my suitor. Though I suppose I would have to pass a law to allow you to wear your shoes indoors."

————

"The Cobbler's Daughter" originally appeared in *MYTHIC Magazine* in September 2018.

WE HAVE NOT ALWAYS BEEN SMALL

———————

"We have not always been small," Apa, the eldest, intones.

"Smol?" asks the tiniest of us. "What's 'smol,' Apa?"

"Not 'smol.' Small." Apa sighs, rustling the pages of his book. "Will you hear my story?"

Most of the time, we don't listen when Apa reads. There's too much fun to be had to listen to old stories. But sometimes, when it's dark and cold, and we are sleepy, we listen.

~

Delilah had been in the world for too long. The point was driven home when her first awareness of an approaching visitor was when he triggered the ensorcelled mirror that showed his heart's desire. Hedy had crafted the mirror to dissuade the numerous fortune seekers, glory seekers, and others who disturbed their solitude.

"What does this one want?" Hedy asked. The witch had snuck up on Delilah, which happened more and more these days. Though Delilah's hearing had been damaged by years of roars, Hedy's eyesight was failing, in spite of her magic. She relied on Delilah to see for her.

Delilah turned to the mirror. The visitor was, predictably, a young man—a prince, by his dress. He embraced a woman, but it was not until the two lovers separated that Delilah recognized the woman as a younger version of her human form, dressed in a flowing white wedding gown.

Her mouth opened and closed several times without sound before Hedy poked her with a trembling, bony finger. "Well, Dee? What does he want?"

"I ... to woo me, I think."

Hedy cackled. "Woo you? Oh, that's rich."

Delilah shook her head. "Why would he think me interested in a puny mortal like him? I have immolated all seven of my dragonkind mates." She spun away from the mirror and stalked up the stairs to the highest tower.

Hedy trailed behind her, dodging Delilah's tail. "What are you going to do, Dee?"

"I'll let him say his piece. But then I'll burn him, like the rest."

From the top of the tower, the prince was as small as an ant. Delilah would not be able to hear him at this distance, and she did so like to hear mortal men scream while their skin sizzled. She flared out her wings and dove toward the ground, enjoying the feel of the wind rushing past her. As she neared the ground, she flapped her wings a single time. The prince stood his ground, to her surprise.

Delilah filled her lungs to speak. But in that gulp of air, she caught something spicy, and she coughed. "What do you want?" she managed to croak.

The prince smiled, wide and crooked, just the sort of smile that Delilah imagined brought mortal women to their knees. "Thank you for the pleasure of your company, Lady Delilah. I have come to ask you for the favor of your hand in marriage."

At least he does not mince words once he's through with the pleasantries. "And why would I want to marry one such as yourself?"

"Because I have studied your long and illustrious history, and I can offer you something you have never had before. How would you like to be a queen?"

"Queen?" Delilah tried to laugh, but the spice that hung in the air turned it into a coughing chuckle instead. "What makes you believe I care for grand titles?"

"It is not so much the title that you desire, Lady Delilah. But I heard a rumor that Iuliana now calls herself a princess, so perhaps now titles are the thing that dragonkind pursue."

Delilah frowned. This prince had done his research. She had never held a title. Mortal titles were unimportant to dragons. Yet hearing Iuliana had acquired a princess-ship made her curious. And perhaps a bit envious, though she would never admit it aloud. "Then you are a king?"

"No, my lady, not a king, but merely a prince."

"An eldest prince, then?"

The prince's gaze darted away. "Alas, I have elder brothers. But were I to come home with a dragoness as my bride, how could I fail to become a king?"

"Filled with ambition, and so certain of himself. What need have I for one such as you? If I wished to become a queen and made my desire known, I would have kings lined up from here to the river to request my hand." Delilah shook her head and tried to take a deep breath. Again, the lingering spice in the air prevented her from taking as much air into her lungs as she wished.

"Perhaps that is true, but I've come here with a plan, and I will not fail." He smirked. "I've noticed you seem to be having trouble breathing. Would you like to know why that is?"

Delilah considered the prince for a long moment. "Since you seem so pleased with yourself, it would be kind of me to ask why before I devour you."

The prince shook his head. "No, you will not devour me either, not when you hear what I have done. Before I came here, I trained myself to eat the hottest peppers in all of the land, the Firebells. And I have eaten nothing but Firebells for the past three years, in preparation. You cannot breathe because my entire body exudes their fire, thus you cannot burn me where I stand. And if you eat me, I will burn in your stomach for years before you are comfortable again."

The prince spoke the truth. The Firebells would not kill her, but they would make her life unpleasant until their effects abated. And now that their stench was in her lungs, she could not take in enough air to produce flames to immolate the prince. She considered her other options. His armor was far too spiky for her to crush him beneath her foot without injuring herself. "You have thought this through," Delilah said. "But what will keep me from batting you beyond the river with my tail?"

"Only the knowledge that I will not be dissuaded from pursuing your hand in marriage, no matter how far away I am sent. I intend for you to be my princess, and one day my queen, Lady Delilah. I have suffered for more than three years for you. You will have me, one way or another."

"I see." Delilah considered the prince. "I require time to think on your offer. Excuse me." Without waiting for a response, she flapped her wings and headed back to the tower where Hedy waited.

From the look on Hedy's face, Delilah did not need to ask her old friend if she had been listening. "Now what do I do?" Delilah asked.

Hedy chuckled. "He's far more prepared than even any of the fortune and glory seekers have ever been. If he'd come for our gold, I'd be inclined to let him cart away as much as he could carry. Heck, I'd even be willing to lay low and pretend he had slain us both." She tapped her chin in thought. "Actually, that's a good way to keep people from coming here. We could fake our deaths. Maybe he'll help."

"You are not helping," Delilah said. "I'll find another way to burn him. My reputation must be maintained, after all, as the Burner of All Things."

"We have oil in the cellar, but I doubt he will stand still for long enough to be doused and have flame set to him." Hedy shook her head. "Firebells for three years. That's astonishing devotion, Dee."

Delilah sighed, still feeling the tickle of the spice in her lungs. "While his guile and dedication are both quite admirable, I have no interest in being his consort and spending what remains of my life as a human woman. After all, he will wish for an heir—" She shuddered. "No thank you. I will not undergo that indignity again."

"Well, if you can't burn him, and you won't marry him, then we're back to either faking our deaths or running away. And my bones are too old for running, Dee. You go if you want to, but I'm going to stay."

Delilah looked at her old friend. They had come from such different beginnings, but now, they were each other's only friend. Sharing the castle with Hedy had been easier than sharing it with any of her mates. They didn't fight over who got to sit on the highest perch. Hedy kept her laboratories deep underground and appreciated the privacy it afforded her. It was a good arrangement, and Delilah didn't want it to change. She worried about what would happen to Hedy if the witch was in the castle alone, forgetting to eat and sleeping all of the time. And she feared what she herself would become on her own.

Fear. That was the answer. "Where did we put the mirror that shows one's deepest fear?"

Hedy frowned. "You told me to break it and grind all of the pieces to dust, because it was flawed. Something about dragons not having fears."

Delilah's shoulders slumped. "I told you I have a temper at times."

"I know," Hedy replied. "That's why I wrapped it up in the cloak of one of those princes you immolated, and tucked it away behind the scullery staircase."

Delilah grinned, which became a much less fearsome expression as she transformed into a human woman. "Then we have another choice. I tell my suitor that before I can marry him, I must take stock of what sort of man he is. And we learn his fears, and use those to drive him away."

~

Dressed in one of her finest gowns of crimson silk, and carrying the enchanted mirror in front of her, Delilah looked very different on her second descent from the castle. The prince's brow furrowed until recognition dawned in him. "My Lady Delilah. The years have been so kind to you."

It was a lie. She bore her signs of age with pride. But human men hated to be reminded of their own mortality, and Hedy loved having the chance to cast a small glamour on her old friend to make her look desirable to the young prince. "My sweet prince. You have not told me your name, your kingdom, nor anything else about you."

"I am Prince Wischard the Indomitable, of the Kingdom of Glortania."

Delilah fought back a laugh. "Of course you are. And these are things I am glad to know. But there is more I must know of you. Something that can be determined by you telling me what you see when you look into this mirror." She turned the silver of the mirror toward Prince Wischard and studied his expression.

Prince Wischard frowned deeply at first, but then his eyes widened, and he raised both his arms to cover his face. "What is this sorcery?" he snarled.

"Tell me what you saw, my prince."

"Foul, evil beasts that are unfit to live within a castle. My dogs will chase them out if you plan to bring cats into our home."

Cats. Delilah had to bite her tongue to keep from laughing this time. The prince's deepest fear was not that his intended bride might decide to devour him in spite of the Firebells in his system. It was small, fluffy, and ridiculously common.

She turned the mirror away from Prince Wischard. "Why my dear, sweet, Prince Wischard. I understand. If you will wait here but a little longer, I will go back in to prepare myself to leave."

Prince Wischard looked at her, eyes narrowed. "You ... you will come with me?"

Delilah smiled at him, but said nothing as she turned and went back into the castle.

Hedy was waiting just inside the doorway. "Cats." She chuckled. "Well, that's an easy one."

"Indeed," Delilah said, shrugging out of her fine gown and setting it aside. "I only wish we had more than me to transform into a cat."

"Think small," Hedy said as she readied her wand.

Delilah imagined herself as the tiniest of cats, little more than a ball of black fluff and blue eyes. Even when the pain of transformation into something so small racked her body, she kept her mind fixed on her desired form.

"It is done," Hedy wheezed, slumping to sit on a moldering divan.

Delilah stretched her paws out in front of her and arched her back. The underside of the divan was at her eye level now. "Thank you, dear friend," she purred, though the words came out clear as day.

Scampering down the front stairs, Delilah saw the prince pacing the yard. He did not notice a creature so small as she stalked across the yard to him, until she brushed up against his leg and chirruped.

"Gah!" He leapt backward, stifling the first sneeze, but then erupting into a fit of sneezes.

Delilah smiled and pounced on the prince's leg, her claws slipping through the chainmail he wore. "Do you not recognize me, sweet Prince Wischard? I thought it fitting that I resume my true form before leaving here with you."

"You are a cat!" he exclaimed, batting her away from his ankles. "I thought you a dragon!"

"I am a shapeshifter," she said. *Technically the truth, if bent a bit to serve my purposes.* "But I am most comfortable in this form. And yet across the land, it is the shape of the dragon that is most feared."

"Perhaps that is true, but—" An enormous sneeze prevented him from saying more.

"Do you not desire a kiss from your beloved?" Delilah used her claws to gain purchase in Prince Wischard's armor, and began to climb toward his face.

"No, no!" he cried. "And I rescind my offer of marriage."

"Oh," Delilah said, letting go of the prince and leaping gracefully to the ground. "Goodbye, then, my sweet prince."

"Goodbye, Lady Delilah." He turned and hurried back to his horse.

Delilah waited in the yard until she could no longer hear the hoofbeats of Prince Wischard's horse. Then she rolled her shoulders, ready to transform back to her true form.

Nothing happened.

"Hedy?" Delilah called out, already racing toward the door. "Hedy, I can't transform!"

Hedy still slumped on the divan, though she opened her eyes as Delilah's small claws clattered across the stone floor. "Can't transform?" She waved her wand, then frowned. "Oh dear."

"Oh dear? What do you mean?"

"The magic's stuck fast, Dee. I'm going to need to do some research to find out how to unstick it."

Delilah blinked at Hedy. "Stuck? No witch's spell should be enough to keep me from my true form."

"No, there should be nothing that can do such. But if you can't shift, then something has gone wrong." She shook her head. "This may take some time."

Delilah climbed up into Hedy's lap and nuzzled Hedy's arm. "What can I do to help?"

Hedy reached down and petted the top of Delilah's head. "Come with me down to my lab. At least now you can do that easily. We'll cover more ground if you help with the research."

~

Ten years later, Hedy and Delilah were no closer to finding a way to transform Delilah back into her dragon form. But the princes had stopped coming to the castle. Instead, the two found themselves visited by cats of all colors and sizes. Delilah learned to speak with them, and some stayed longer than others. One, in particular, a young tom who called himself Romeo, stayed with her as she bore him litter after litter of kittens.

At night, when Hedy retired from the lab, Delilah followed her up to her room and curled up in bed with her old friend, keeping the witch warm and safe through the night.

As the years had passed, Delilah became content in her new form. She was young again, rejuvenated. And she realized the truth of what magic Hedy should pursue.

"Turn yourself into a cat," Delilah suggested, watching her old friend try and fail to turn the page in the book she was reading.

"What good would I be to you if I were a cat?" Hedy sighed.

"We two could be the fiercest cats in all the land. We could leave our castle and find a nice, warm house where we can live out the rest of our days. Somewhere where they will keep our bellies full and our ears scratched. It would be a good life. And better for your old bones than a drafty, damp castle."

Hedy sighed again, but this time, the sound was not one of frustration. "You do make it sound pleasant."

"Will you, then?"

"You are happy, being a cat?"

Delilah hesitated, thinking back on her long life. She nodded. "It is good. And so much easier than defending our castle against the fortune seekers and the glory seekers and whoever else comes to bother us in our old age."

Hedy smiled. "Then I think perhaps I shall join you in that nice warm house. But I think we must find one near a field, with plenty of mice."

Delilah's eyes sparkled. "Oh yes, plenty of mice."

~

"And that, my children, is why we are so full of fire and fight," Apa said, his voice now softer than a whisper.

All of us had moved close to him as he read his story, so we could catch every word he offered up, eyes wide. Without warning, Apa lashed out and tapped the tiniest on her nose. "Until the very end."

The tiniest hissed, immediately on all fours, her back arched, fur standing on end, and tail whipping back and forth.

Apa told the truth. We are the descendants of the dragons who have been long gone from this world. We have not always been small.

DRY SPELL

———————

Marya was still in the parlor when Master Laurence and his friends retired there after dinner. The windows gleamed in the twilight, all but the one she had yet to scrub. The three men paid her no heed, and she knelt to move her bucket, the water now gray. Before she resumed her work, one of Master Laurence's friends said something that caught her attention: "*messecer a tutus illus.*"

She could not comprehend the words at first, despite the nagging feeling they gave her. But then she recognized her confusion. The language was not her native Cousmoshi, but Atmani. The man had said "slaughter all of them."

Marya rose from her crouched position on the floor, and Master Laurence looked up. "Ah, Mariah. Did Eleanor send you in?"

Marya. She corrected her Master only in her thoughts. The memory of the lashing she had received the only time she had dared correct him aloud still stung. She shook her head in response.

"Well, since you are here, bring us three glasses of rum."

"Of course, sir." Marya curtseyed before making her way to the sideboard. The conversation returned to Atmani.

"How certain are you that this ritual of yours will work?" one of the men asked.

Marya glanced over her shoulder and identified him as Holclair, one of the nearby farmstead owners. She recognized a hint of a Cousmoshi accent to his speech that made her long for her distant homeland.

The other man, Zurvuld, replied. "It worked in the outpost to the south."

Marya carried three glasses of rum to the men, placing each on one of the small marble-topped tables beside their chairs. Master Laurence rolled a thin cigar between his hands, not looking up when he set it aside to take up his glass. "And it might have saved Lewes Outpost, had we not balked. Holclair, it is our only hope."

Holclair sighed. "Perhaps. But can we not wait out the season? Rain may yet come."

Marya frowned as she turned away from the conversation. She had been at this outpost for near two years, and had heard Lewes Outpost spoken of only in the faintest whispers. But she understood the lack of rain all too well. Every time a breeze blew, it brought with it a shower of dirt, scoured from the baked earth. In all the time she had spent in Obun, it had rained fewer times than she could count on one hand.

Zurvuld must have spoken too softly for her to hear, but Master Laurence replied to both of his friends. "Gentlemen, we have seen the portents. We cannot just 'wait out the season.' If we do not act now, we will not have another opportunity. And if our crops fail, the winter will be long and hard for all of us."

"When, then, shall we proceed?" Holclair asked.

"Two nights hence." Master Laurence struck a match and lit the end of his cigar.

The stench of the tobacco was acrid and foul, nothing like the kind Marya's grandfather used to fill his pipe in Cousmos. She remembered the faint spicy scent, the prickle of his whiskers against her cheek, but as she took a breath of the parlor air, the distasteful odor tickled at her nose instead.

Marya coughed, and Master Laurence looked up, as though he had forgotten about her. He switched back to Obic. "Ah, yes, thank you. You are dismissed."

"Wait," Zurvuld said. Returning to Atmani, he stared at Marya as he spoke. "Do you understand Atmani?"

Marya opened her mouth to reply "no," but bit her tongue before a sound escaped. She frowned, furrowing her brow. "I beg your pardon, sir. Could you repeat that? I did not understand what you asked."

Zurvuld shook his head. "Never you mind, dearie." He shooed her with a wave of his hand.

Marya returned to the window to collect her bucket and cleaning rags, and the men continued their conversation. She breathed shallowly, not wanting to inhale the cigar smoke, and frightened to make too much noise.

"Two nights hence," Holclair repeated. "We shall make the necessary sacrifice." He sighed. "But I shall miss this place."

~

Marya slipped into her room on tiptoe. Katrin's slight frame lay beneath the sheet on their shared bed. Marya sat on the edge of the bed and reached beneath it for her boots.

"You smell like cigars," Katrin murmured.

"The Master and his friends are smoking in the parlor."

"Did they want you to dance for them again?"

"No. They were talking about something different. I need to see the Constable."

The sheet stiffened beneath Marya as Katrin bolted upright. "Why in the goddess's name would you do that, Marya?"

Marya hushed Katrin. Some of the other house girls stirred on the other side of the thin walls. "The gentlemen were talking in Atmani about murder ... to slaughter all of us. They didn't know I understood them."

"So you're going to walk to the Constable's house and tell him you heard our Master plotting to kill us? What do you expect the Constable to do?"

Marya frowned. Katrin was right. If a master wanted to beat his slaves to death, no one would stop him. Why would it be any different if he planned to kill them in some other fashion? But this felt different, somewhere in Marya's gut. "Well, I can't sit by idly and do nothing, either."

"Yes, you can," Katrin insisted. "Did they say when this slaughter will occur?"

"The night after tomorrow."

Katrin's dark eyes flashed. "Then after dinner that day, we'll sneak off into the woods. They won't notice we're missing if they're rounding up all of the other slaves."

Marya's jaw dropped. "What about the rest? What about Cecily and Joan?" She paused, staring straight at Katrin. "What about Oliver?"

Katrin chewed at her lip for a moment. "Yes, bringing Oliver is a good idea. He can protect us. But we can't bring everyone. They'll just slow us down and make it more obvious that we're escaping."

"I'm not going if you're not going to try to bring everyone with us," Marya said, shaking her head.

"Then you'll be slaughtered, Marya."

"No, I'll find a way to stop this." She tugged her boots on. "I'm going to the Constable. I'll think of something to tell him while I walk."

~

By the time Marya reached Constable Arn's house, she had not settled on a plan that would likely work. Everything she had thought of had been variations on somehow convincing the Constable she and her fellow slaves were important and worth saving. But Marya knew as well as Katrin did that such was not true in this area. Whether the slaves were from Atman, Riprat, or elsewhere made no difference to the masters.

The sound of a rifle cocking froze Marya in her tracks. "Well what do we have here, boys?" The voice bore a thick drawl, and the slurred together words that suggested its owner had been drinking.

Marya curtseyed, bowing her head low. "I come from Master Laurence to speak with the Constable. Is he at home?"

"Master Laurence don't send pretty *taama* girls like you to run messages for him. That is, unless the message is that he's gonna entertain the Constable with the likes of you."

Marya bristled at the slur. The Cousmoshi had long been called *taama*, and the rumors of their seductive dancing and witchcraft had followed them to the outposts. "I was not sent to dance," Marya murmured, speaking quietly to hide her anger. "Just to convey a message."

"Well, why don't you tell me the message, and I'll give it to the Constable for you?" The bearer of the voice tucked one finger under Marya's chin and pulled it up until she was looking him in the eyes. The stench of cheap alcohol rolled off him in waves.

"I appreciate your offer," she replied, fluttering her eyelashes so she no longer locked eyes with him. "Master Laurence said it was of utmost importance that I speak with the Constable directly."

"You talk real fancy for a serving girl. What's your name?"

"Marya."

"Mar-di-a?" The man's drawl elongated her name into something almost unrecognizable. "That's a fancy name, too."

"Hey, Brod," another voice said. "Why don't you go get the Constable and leave her here with us? We'll make sure nothin' happens while you're gone."

The guffaws of the other men nearby finally made Marya realize how much of a mistake she had made in coming here. She could not defend herself against even one of these men if they wished her ill. She looked back up at the one they had called Brod. "Please, will you take me with you to speak with Constable Arn?"

Brod shook his head. "No, I ain't going to fetch the Constable, and I ain't going to take you to see him, neither. You can tell me the message you have for him, or you can go home and tell Master Laurence to send one of his usual messengers, tomorrow."

Marya had not decided on what to tell the Constable if she was able to meet with him. She had even less of an idea as to what to tell his men to tell him.

Brod stepped closer to her. "C'mon, *taama*. What's the message?"

"Please tell Constable Arn that Master Laurence requests the pleasure of his company two nights hence," she blurted out. Perhaps if the Constable was there, the slaughter and the ritual the men had spoken of would not take place.

"Two nights hence?" Brod asked, his brow furrowing. "The Constable was already planning to be at the festival then."

Marya felt chilled to the bone in spite of the summer heat that still lingered after dark. "He ... oh, I ... my apologies, then, for taking up so much of your time." She curtseyed again and hurried away, nearly oblivious to the catcalls and shouts of "come dance for us, *taama*" that followed her all the way down the drive.

When she reached the main road, she paused a moment to regain control of her breathing. If the Constable already planned to be at a festival on the night of the ritual, then he not only knew of the plan, but also supported it. And if that were the case, then the likelihood of any of the slaves surviving the slaughter was very small indeed.

~

27

Katrin was waiting for Marya at the back of the big house when she returned from her failed errand to the Constable's. She didn't even bother to ask Marya how it went, but grabbed her by the hand and dragged her inside.

Not until they reached the library did Katrin release her grip on Marya. "I found the Master's book," Katrin hissed under her breath.

"What book?"

"I think it's a book of magic." She peeked back out into the hallway before locking the door.

Marya gasped. If anyone were to discover them in Master Laurence's library, with the door locked, whatever the men were planning for two nights hence would be the least of their worries. She bolted toward the door, but Katrin stopped her.

"I can't read the language it's in," Katrin whispered. "And we can't take the book anywhere else."

Marya shook her head. "I don't know how to read. Are there any drawings?"

"There are a few." Katrin's face paled. "Some of them look like instructions on how to stab people."

"Master Holclair said something about a sacrifice. Let me see the book."

Katrin pulled a large tome off of the shelf. The cover was dark brown, mottled with lighter spots, and singed on the top edge. The binding creaked as Katrin opened the book on Master Laurence's desk.

Marya coughed from the dust the book released, but leaned forward to see what Katrin had found. "How did you find this?"

"The Master was reading it when he called me to bring him more rum. He must have known I can't understand it."

Marya looked at the drawings Katrin had mentioned, gruesome depictions of men drawn and quartered, and others with strange symbols carved into their flesh. She scanned the words on the page, but they meant nothing to her. "*Messcer a tutus illus*," she muttered. "Do you see anything like that in here?"

"How ... alright, '*tutus*' sounds easy enough." Katrin bent over the page and pointed to one of the words. "Here it is."

"Good. That means 'all.' What does that one say?" She pointed at the next word.

"I-L-L-U-S."

Marya sighed. "I don't know how to spell words in Obic or Atmani." Her gaze flickered across the page. "Wait, that there, in red. Can you read that?"

"Something about a ritual. Is that right?"

"*Retul*," Marya said. "I suppose they sound similar. What else?"

"Uh, *deedee seer comple* ... I think that's completed?"

Marya puzzled over the words Katrin said. "*Dede?*" She suggested.

"Sure, maybe."

"The ritual must be completed ... That's good! What's next?"

"*Ents ta la* ... I think it's your name. Marya nos."

"*Madianosh*," Marya said, certain about her roommate's confusion this time. "The ritual must be completed before midnight." She smiled. "That means all we need to do is make sure it gets delayed or stopped. Once it's past midnight ... well, I suspect it will be too late."

Katrin frowned. "What makes two nights hence so important?"

Marya looked out the window. "Full moon. Is there anything ... *luna*. Do you see that anywhere?"

"Yes, *luna eyana?*"

"I don't know what that means. But it's something about the moon." Marya looked back at the page. "So maybe it's the full moon. But there must be something special about this full moon."

"It's midsummer," Katrin said, her face growing pale. "Or it will be, in two days."

"Good, then if we can stop the ritual, they won't be able to try again." Marya glanced at the page once more. "What is that word?"

Katrin turned her attention back to the book. "Myrr ... Myrrka—" She gasped. "I mustn't say it! It will bring us bad luck!"

Marya frowned. "Is it important?"

"I don't know. It might be. There's a place where they say everyone vanished. They were there, and then gone. And there was a word, carved into a tree, and no one knows why. But that word, it's supposed to be the worst kind of luck."

"What are the other words near it?"

"Umm, *fend ... epota ... quius?*"

"End of the drought?" Marya murmured. "End of the drought!"

"Shh!" Katrin said. "We mustn't be found out, remember."

29

"Of course," Marya said. "I think I've learned enough. We're going to need some help."

~

In the morning, Marya and Katrin sought out Oliver.

"How many men are on your crew?" Katrin asked.

Oliver raised one eyebrow, but said, "A dozen."

"We need you to spread the word," Marya said. "Tomorrow evening, there's to be some sort of gathering. We need as many slaves as possible to rise up just before midnight."

"You're planning a slave revolt now, are you, Marya?" He chuckled. "And dragging Katrin into it as well?"

Marya took a step closer to Oliver and lowered her voice. "If we do nothing, a lot of slaves will be killed. Maybe all of us."

"There's no guarantee that us rising up won't have the same outcome." He looked at Katrin. "You sure about this?"

Katrin sighed and crossed her arms over her chest. "I wouldn't be here if I wasn't. Just trust Marya, please. She's trying to help."

"Alright. What's the gathering, then?"

"I don't know for certain. Perhaps a midsummer's festival."

"That's why they've had a crew building in town then, I suspect."

"I have to go into town today," Katrin said. "I can spread the word to them."

"Good," Marya said. "Oliver, try to get the message to as many of the fieldhands as you can. I'll talk to the house staff. Katrin, you talk to anyone you see who can be trusted. That goes for you, too, Oliver. If you think they might let our plan slip, don't tell them. We'll just have to hope we can sweep them up on our way."

~

Early the next afternoon, Master Laurence came into the laundry, where Marya and Katrin sweated over huge cauldrons of boiling water and clothing. "Follow me."

His two simple words were enough to make both women stop what they were doing and walk behind him out into the courtyard, which baked in the hot summer sun. Several other household slaves waited there, looking as confused as Marya felt. Holclair and Zurvuld regarded the group, along with Master Laurence.

Marya leaned toward Katrin, but felt Zurvuld's gaze settle on her. She held her tongue, but looked at her friend, trying to convey her thoughts with just her eyes. *We need to run.*

Master Laurence spoke up before Katrin reacted to Marya's gaze. "You are to accompany my friends to the town center, in order to complete the preparations for this evening's celebration. You need take nothing with you. Constable Arn's men will accompany you."

Now Katrin's eyes grew wide, as she realized the meaning of Marya's expression. "We need to get word to the others," she murmured as the Constable's men grouped the women closer together.

"There's no time," Marya said. One of the Constable's men had produced a long chain with manacles, which he began to place on the ankles of the other slaves. Another stood by, rifle in hand, his gaze narrow as he watched the women who had not yet been shackled. "We can only hope we find some other opportunity to escape."

As they clamped the iron around her ankle, she remembered all too vividly the first time she had been chained in such a fashion, in Atman. She found it odd to hope this would not be the last time she felt such a sensation. But being chained was not as final of a fate as death.

The walk to town took twice as long as usual with the women all chained to each other. While the other women had clustered into small groups along the chain, Marya knew few of the others, aside from Katrin.

"None of these women know of our plan," Katrin muttered to Marya, confirming what she had suspected.

Marya listened to the chatter of the others. She recognized few of their words. And while it was likely that all of the slaves spoke a little bit of Obic, so did the Constable's men. She doubted they had any other language in common, which made adding them to the plan all the more difficult. "We still have to try," she said. "Oliver will bring the others to the festival."

Arriving in town, Marya realized she might have spoken too soon. Oliver and a group of other male slaves from Master Laurence's farmstead were in a similar predicament of imprisonment, though the chain they were attached to had more widely spaced manacles. They worked on a partially built dais, shaped like a multi-pointed star, which Marya recognized from the book she and Katrin had found.

Marya tried to catch Oliver's gaze, but he kept his head down as he hammered thick nails into place. She glanced at the other workers, but saw no one else who they had spoken to about their plan. "We're going to have to find another way to stop them," she murmured to Katrin.

"I think we're going to be right in the thick of things," Katrin replied. She gestured at the dais with her chin. "Thirteen points. Thirteen girls. We're the sacrifice."

Marya froze as she counted both the points on the dais and the girls attached to the chain. Katrin was right. Marya looked around, eyes wild. "We must stop this."

"Well, they can't sacrifice us if we're dead before they start," Katrin said with a shrug.

"What good will that do us? The point is to survive!"

Katrin shrugged again. "We could kill one of the others, then."

Marya shook her head. "I don't want to kill anyone!"

A firm grip on her arm drew her attention. Brod pinched the delicate skin on the underside of her upper arm. "What are you talking about killing people for?"

In a panic, the words flowed out of her. "They're going to kill all of us tonight!"

"And?"

Marya's heart sank. She had not expected a different response, no matter how much she hoped. "Oh," she whispered in reply, dropping her gaze to the ground.

Brod pulled her closer to him. Even in the middle of the afternoon, the stench of alcohol still clung to him. "Keep quiet. If you cause a panic, I'll kill you myself. There's plenty of girls we can replace you with." He released her arm and shoved her toward Katrin. "Tell your friend, too."

Marya kept her gaze averted, but her blood boiled. She would keep quiet for now, but even his threats could not keep her from her plan, with or without anyone else.

Katrin wrapped her arms around Marya. "Are you alright?"

"I'll be fine," Marya replied. "But we aren't killing anyone. We stick to the plan. All we have to do is cause enough of a stir that the ritual is disrupted and isn't finished by midnight."

"And hope they don't decide to kill us anyway," Katrin muttered under her breath.

~

As the festival progressed, Marya realized she had no way of telling the time beyond the town crier announcing the hours. She hoped the organizers of the ritual might be distracted enough to forget to start things on time.

Master Laurence checked his pocket watch and conferred with Zurvuld and Holclair. Then he raised his hands until the crowd quieted. "Ladies and gentlemen. I would like to ask you all to bear with us for a few minutes. There's something that must be done this evening."

Marya seized the opportunity. Ducking her head so the movement of her mouth was not apparent, she called out in a deep voice, "Come now, Laurence! Surely this can wait!"

Master Laurence's gaze darted across the crowd, but others had taken up her plea. As calls for the continuation of the celebration rang out, the three men on the dais consulted briefly. Master Laurence nodded at the Constable, and Brod tugged the chain connecting the thirteen women.

"We're going to have a little additional entertainment," Master Laurence said as the first of the women reached the dais.

Marya looked around for any sign that Oliver or any of the others from the farmstead were ready to act. None of them were in sight, but she had only moments before she would be pulled onto the dais. "Now! Now is the time!"

No one responded to her call, other than Katrin, who grabbed the girl on the other side of her around the waist. "Don't go up there! They're going to kill us!"

Katrin's words spurred the other chained women into a panic. Those who were already on the dais tried to get down, though they moved in as many directions as they had limbs. The women beyond Marya, Katrin, and the woman Katrin was holding also tried to flee, but their flight had no organization either.

Marya linked her arm through Katrin's and began to pull her friend away from the center of town. Between the two of them, many of the other women started moving in the right direction. The few who were still in a panic were dragged along by the force of the others' movement, or picked up by their neighbors.

"Stop them!" Master Laurence shrieked.

Brod moved to intercept the women, stopping directly in front of Marya. "Get back on the dais, *taama*."

"No," she said, quiet but firm. Raising her voice, she continued. "These men want to kill us, because they believe they can use magic to change the weather. They're practicing witchcraft. Who will stand for this?"

Murmurs erupted throughout the crowd. Marya's accusation was serious, but also plausible enough to be believed.

"Nonsense," Master Laurence said, forcing a chuckle. "We only want to have these ladies entertain you. Some might call it a rain dance, but don't we need the rain?"

The murmurs shifted to approving, with cries of "yes" and "without a doubt" resounding.

Marya reached into the depths of her memory and began to chant a nursery rhyme from her childhood, in Cousmoshi. The words were nearly nonsensical, but they were also words few in the crowd had ever heard before. Eyes grew wide as she released her grip on Katrin's arm and began to draw fake sigils in the air.

"She's a *taama*!" someone exclaimed. "She would know if they're going to work witchcraft!"

Marya paused in her recitation, making an elaborate design in the air before her, and whispered to Katrin. "Keep the line moving. We need to get out of here before they decide to burn me instead of the masters."

Katrin nodded in response, her eyes wide with the same fear the townspeople showed. Marya had never given her friend any indication that she knew magic, primarily because she did not. But the tales of *taama* magic were enough to make the people around Marya assume the worst, even if they trusted her.

Even the masters, the Constable, and Brod had backed away from Marya as she chanted and gestured. Her grandmother, a devout follower of the Old Ways in life, was sure to be turning over in her grave in far off Cousmos.

In spite of the tension throughout the town square, the crier did his job. "Twelve o'clock is upon us. Praise be to the gods, Old and New, for seeing us through another day."

Marya released a deep breath. It was too late for the masters to complete the ritual now.

Brod glared at Marya and reached for his rifle. "You're gonna pay, *taama*. One way or another."

Oliver stepped between Marya and Brod, brandishing a pitchfork. "This may not stop you from shooting me, but there are plenty more of these where this one came from." He turned his head to the side. "Get out of here. Take Katrin and run. We'll find you."

Several of Oliver's fellow farmhands, armed primarily with farming implements, interposed themselves between the slave women and the townspeople.

Marya could no longer even see Brod. She grabbed Katrin's hand tightly and pulled her and the other women toward the tree line. She could not resist shouting one last thing as the slaves made their way out of the town square. "A curse be upon your house, Laurence. May all remember you gave the lives of your slaves no regard." She pointed at him, making a gesture with her other hand.

Clouds slipped across the moon, obscuring its light. Marya was not the cause of it, but the effect was perfect, as the slaves slipped away into the trees.

STORMBRINGER

Tam lingered as the field hands boarded the wagon back to the village. Mammy Berga had her spinning wheel set up on her porch and worked there in the shade. Tam cast one last glance at the wagon before gathering up his nerve to approach Mammy Berga.

People said Mammy Berga had been beautiful in her day, but that was decades previous. Now, her thinning white hair stayed knotted tightly at the base of her neck, and wrinkles covered every inch of exposed flesh. In the five years Tam had worked on Mammy Berga's farm, he had spoken with the woman about the same number of times.

"Evening, Mammy," he said, repeating himself louder when she did not respond to him. She finally nodded, but her attention remained on the woolen thread her spinning wheel produced. "It's a real scorcher today, ain't it?"

Mammy Berga's gaze flicked up for a second. "Yup."

"Uh, some of the boys think we'll have rain before morning."

The spinning wheel stopped and Mammy Berga set down her fluffy unspun wool. She scanned the cloudless horizon before responding. "Mayhap."

A trickle of sweat rolled down the back of Tam's neck, not from the heat, but from his nerves. "Rain would be good."

Mammy Berga sighed and shook her head. "Tam, the wagon's about to leave. Now I don't think you're here just to chat about the weather with an old woman. What's on your mind, boy?"

Tam cleared his throat and gnawed at the inside of his lip. "I, well, I've come to ask you, to ask for Ellie ... to marry Ellie's hand." As soon as the words had left his mouth, Tam cursed himself for screwing up such a simple question. "May I ask your daughter for her hand in marriage?" he blurted.

A smile turned up the edges of Mammy Berga's lips. "I see. Have you spoken to Ellie about this proposition?"

"Yes. Well, in a roundabout sort of way."

"And has she seemed favorable toward such a roundabout suggestion?"

"Er, well, I haven't asked, exactly. Not in so many words, at least." Tam scratched his head as he spoke, sure that a sheepish grin had attached itself to his face despite his best efforts.

Mammy Berga leaned back in her chair and looked at Tam for a long while. Finally, she nodded and took up her spinning again. "Mayhap you ought to go ask her in so many words. If she'll have you, then that's all the permission you'll need."

Tam restrained himself from leaping with joy. "Thank you, Mammy Berga. She out in the orchard?"

"Mayhap," Mammy Berga replied. "Mayhap."

~

Tam ran nearly all the way to the orchard. As he neared the place where the fields gave way to the short trees, he slowed his pace and tried to rein in his breathing. He began rehearsing what he planned to say. The words came smoothly—he had practiced them in front of the mirror for months.

The sun hovered at the horizon, blinding anyone who looked toward it. Tam closed his eyes, stretching out his arms to either side as he and Ellie had done when they were children playing hide and seek in the orchard. The tips of the branches would warn him long before he ran into any of the trees. The afterimage of the sun lingered on the inside of his eyelids.

His fingertips brushed a tree branch, and he opened his eyes again. The branch was long and straggly, jutting out into the pathway between trees. He stepped around it and noticed the sunlight pierced his eyes less now. A thin band of clouds had appeared on the horizon, and diffused the light into the brilliant colors of a prairie sunset.

Tam smiled at the perfect beauty of the setting. "Just the place for a marriage proposal," he murmured to himself. He looked around, trying to catch a glimpse of Ellie. She had been wearing blue when he spotted her at lunch.

Soft blue made a stunning counterpoint against the white of a fine pair of trousers, framed on either side by dark brown tree trunks. Tam hesitated behind a thicker tree. He heard a man's voice, but could not discern the words. But Ellie's soft laughter was unmistakable. Tam's heart lurched in his chest.

He hazarded another look. The man's entire suit was bright white, and his skin was not much darker. Tam wondered if the man was a ghost, perhaps Ellie's pappy, who had died when Ellie was a little girl. But then he caught a glimpse of the man's hair, jet black and loose around his shoulders. A few strands danced in the breeze, and Tam knew the man was no ghost. The man slid a hand to the small of Ellie's back, and Tam looked away.

He cursed himself under his breath. How could he have been so stupid to believe a girl like Ellie had no beaus? True, she was nearer to thirty than twenty, but she was still more beautiful than most of the unmarried girls in the village.

A moment later, Tam peeked out from behind the tree. Ellie was alone, picking up a basket of peaches. Her brow was furrowed, and she chewed at her lower lip. Tam hesitated. Ellie's face did not look like that of a woman whose beloved had just left. That alone propelled him from his hiding place.

"Evening, Ellie."

She looked up and smiled. "Tam! What are you doing out here? Haven't the others all gone back to the village?"

Tam nodded. "Who was that?"

"Who was who?"

"The man you were talking to."

Ellie's mouth worked silently, her lips forming the words "You can't" before she spoke. "There wasn't anyone here, Tam. You must have been out in the sun too long today."

"Mayhap," he replied. "Can I carry those peaches back to the house for you?"

"Well, sure!" She handed him the basket, her gaze lingering on him. "So why didn't you go back to the village with the others?"

"Oh, I—" Tam stammered, then shrugged. "I noticed you hadn't come back from the orchard yet. Your mammy asked me to come out and check on you, if it wasn't too much trouble."

Ellie smiled. "That's awfully sweet of you, Tam. Especially since now you'll be walking back to the village alone."

"It's no trouble. It's already cooling off."

"Likely cool off more when the rain comes."

Tam glanced back over his shoulder at the clouds that now turned the fading light to amber. "A little rain never hurt me."

~

Tam's clothes were plastered to his skin by the time he got home, soaked clear through. He stopped outside the door long enough to remove his boots and socks.

His sister, Brina, looked him up and down as he walked in. "How far did you walk before the storm started?"

"I got about to the end of Mammy Berga's property."

Brina shook her head. "Go find something dry to wear while I get the clothesline strung up."

Tam nodded his thanks and did as she told him. He came back into the main room and tried to hand Brina his clothes.

"You're helping with this, Tam. You've got to learn how to help out around the house if you're going to marry Ellie." Brina paused and looked at him. "I assume that's why you took your time getting home tonight?"

Tam sighed. "Yes and no."

"What sort of answer is that? Did she turn you down?"

"Not exactly, no. I didn't ask."

"What? Why not?"

Tam chewed at his thumb before telling Brina what he had seen in the orchard while they hung up his wet clothes.

"And?" was her only response when he finished.

"And nothing. If she's got another beau, I'm not going to ask her to marry me."

"But you said she looked upset, or confused, when he left. So maybe he wasn't a beau."

"Who else would go out into the orchard, dressed like a dandy, other than someone who wants to court Ellie?" Tam wailed.

"Someone from the city? Maybe a relative? What does it matter? If he were her beau, she wouldn't keep it quiet. She'd have told you."

"Why?"

"Because you've known her since you were old enough to realize there were people in the world other than your family. And because you've been her friend for just as long." Brina paused and

40

glared at Tam. "The day you met her, you came running into the house and told me 'I just met the girl I'm going to marry.' You've waited long enough, Tam. Go ask her."

Tam glanced out the window. "Tonight?"

Brina had already pulled his still wet clothes down from the line. "Yes, tonight. May as well put all this back on. You're just going to get drenched again."

"Do you think Rav will mind if I take his horse?"

"He's down at the pub. He'll never notice."

Tam hesitated. "I think I'll stop in and check with him. Have a pint, maybe."

Brina shoved Tam's clothes into his arms. "No. Straight to Ellie's with you."

~

The storm showed Tam no mercy on his ride back to Ellie's house. At least the rain felt warmer on this trip.

As he rode around the last bend before the house, Ellie's silhouette, outlined by the lights inside, lingered on the porch. He nudged the horse with his heel, but it maintained its slow pace. Tam leapt down and tugged at the reins. He debated letting the horse stand in the middle of the road, but he'd face his brother-in-law's wrath if anything happened to it.

"What are you doing out?" Ellie called out when he neared the porch. "It's pouring down rain!"

"I came back to talk to you."

Ellie crossed her arms over her chest. "What if I don't want to talk to you?"

Tam looked up from the wet reins he was trying to knot around the porch rail. "Why not?"

"I talked to Mammy when I came in. She didn't send you out to walk me back from the orchard. She said you had something to ask me about."

"I did," Tam admitted.

"And?"

"That's why I came back."

Ellie's posture remained the same. "So, ask then."

Tam walked up the stairs to the covered porch. "I can't ask you while you're angry with me, Ellie."

"What made you decide you couldn't ask me in the orchard?"

Tam hesitated. "I thought I saw you talking to a man. I thought—"

Ellie's arms dropped to her sides as she looked away from Tam. Her brow furrowed, and she began chewing at her lip, as she had after the man left the orchard. When she spoke again, her voice was barely audible over the pouring rain. "You saw him? You actually saw him?"

Tam nodded.

"I'm not angry with you, Tam. I'm confused. But I want you to ask me your question."

Tam reached for Ellie's hands. She gave them freely, but did not turn her face to look at him. He sighed. "If you already know what I'm going to ask you, and you want me to ask, then why do you look so sad?"

Ellie hesitated a long time before she answered. "Because I can't say yes."

"Why not? Is it because of that man?"

She finally looked at him. "That man ... doesn't exist. I don't understand why you can see him."

Tam shrugged. "I don't know. But I did. And there's something you're not telling me. About him, about something." He paused and changed his approach, dropping to one knee in front of her. "Ellie, I want to marry you. I've wanted to marry you since we were children. I've waited half my life to finally get up the nerve to ask, but I'm asking now. So will you marry me?"

Tam felt splashes on his upturned face. But the porch roof had not sprung a leak. Ellie's eyes had. He clambered to a standing position and enveloped her in a clumsy hug. "Oh, Ellie. I don't want to make you cry. Tell me what I can do. Tell me how I can make this better."

Ellie's body shook with sobs for several long minutes. Finally, she sniffled and looked at him. "I think we'd better go inside and talk to Mammy. After you've heard us out, then you can decide if your offer still stands."

~

Mammy Berga had moved her spinning wheel into the house, beside the fire. She took in Tam and Ellie's appearances and chuckled as she rose from her seat. "Tam, get over here by this fire before you catch your death. Ellie, go fetch your bedspread and another chair."

Ellie nodded and hurried out of the room. Mammy Berga turned back to Tam as he stood in front of the fire, grateful for the warmth. She shook her head and chuckled again. "Couldn't ask her this afternoon, could you, boy?"

"Mammy Berga, when I went out to the orchard, Ellie was talking to a man. She's confused about why I can see him."

Mammy Berga raised her eyebrows. "Ah. And what has she told you about The Man?"

The final two words of Mammy Berga's question struck Tam as odd. They sounded like a proper name, no different from Tam or Ellie. "The Man?" he asked.

"Well, that's what we call him," Ellie said as she returned to the room. "It's not really what he is, though."

Mammy Berga took the chair from Ellie and draped the bedspread across the tops. "Get you out of those wet clothes, Tam."

Tam flushed but did as he was told. Ellie turned slightly away from him, but she looked at him out of the corner of her eye. Her mouth was turned up in a smile as she watched, which Tam took as a good sign. As he removed the last of his clothes, Mammy Berga wrapped the bedspread around him. It smelled of fresh air, sunlight, and peach blossoms—like Ellie.

Mammy Berga gestured toward the other chair, and Tam sat, carefully arranging the blanket around him. Relieved of his wet clothes, in front of the fire, and wrapped in Ellie's comforter, his mood improved considerably.

"Ellie's right," Mammy Berga said, continuing the conversation as though Tam had not stripped naked in the midst of it. "The Man is no man. Some would call him a devil or an evil spirit. As far as the spirit world goes, he's the ruler of this land. What he wants, he gets."

"And he wants Ellie?"

"In a manner of speaking, yes. You know the stories of Lady Anda?"

Tam nodded. Every child had heard the tales of how this place had been a barren wasteland until the coming of Lady Anda.

"Before she was Lady Anda, Bringer of Storms, she was a girl called Andie. When she grew into a woman, she became Anda. And that's when she made a deal with The Man. Every month, she would make a sacrifice of her woman's blood to him. In exchange, he would release his hold on the clouds, which he had kept from the land for so long."

Ellie spoke up. "Lady Anda was my great grandmammy, many generations back. After she made the deal with The Man, she realized she couldn't continue the arrangement forever. So she made another deal with him. For the span of one year, the monthly sacrifice would be suspended, while she bore a child. The Man held back the clouds for that year, to ensure she upheld her end of the bargain.

"Anda bore a daughter, and when her daughter was thirteen years old, she became the Stormbringer. It's been passed down the line. Always a daughter, always the Stormbringer, always making a monthly sacrifice to The Man, except for the year of drought while she bears the next Stormbringer."

When Ellie finished speaking, Tam remained quiet for a while. The story seemed fantastical, but many of the stories in their land had origins in fact. So for the Stormbringer to be the great grandmammy of his oldest friend hardly seemed a stretch. "Who sires the daughter?"

"Whatever man the Stormbringer marries," Ellie replied.

"Then doesn't that mean that you must marry someone?"

"Eventually, yes. There was a time when all the Stormbringers married young, and had their daughters early. It meant some of them had normal lives later on. But Mammy—" She lowered her voice to a whisper. "Mammy thought there might be a way out of this deal. I've been trying to find a way to break the cycle."

"Oh," Tam said. "But if you wait too long—"

"It's a risk, yes. Mammy almost did wait too long." Ellie looked wistfully toward Mammy. "Pappy was fifty years old when I was born. The year of drought made Pappy take ill. He never really recovered afterward."

Tam looked at both of the women. "I wish there was a way for me to help. Not just because I want to marry Ellie."

"You can't," Mammy Berga snapped. "This is our burden."

"Mammy! What if there is a way? Tam can see The Man. There must be something special about him."

Mammy Berga shook her head. "Some of the Stormbringers who had their daughters early had other children later. Tam must be descended from one of the other lines of Anda. There are plenty of people around who are. None of them have ever happened out into the orchard while one of the Stormbringers was talking to The Man."

"But if there are other descendants, then there are other female descendants." Tam thought for a moment. "Brina! My sister is descended from Anda as well. She could make the sacrifice in Ellie's place."

"Doesn't work like that, boy. It has to be the first born daughter of a first born daughter, all the way back to Anda. Brina isn't one of us."

"Well, we've never tried it," Ellie admitted. "But Brina would have to agree to this first."

Mammy Berga shook her head. "Even if it worked, it wouldn't solve the larger problem. Someone is always bound to being the Stormbringer. Ellie, you may as well marry Tam now, while you're still young. There's time to do the research while your daughter grows. Mayhap you can break the cycle before it becomes her time."

Tam nodded. "I want you to decide if you want to marry now or later." He paused, grimacing. "Or never. But tell me, what have you found so far in your research?"

"Not much," Ellie admitted. "A few old diaries and some drawings."

"May I see them?" Tam asked.

Ellie shared a look with Mammy Berga, then nodded. "I suppose so. Maybe a fresh pair of eyes can find something we've missed."

~

Tam's neck was stiff from bending over the collection of books and papers Ellie and Mammy Berga had walked him through. It was just as Ellie said—random bits of information other Stormbringers had committed to paper. The drawings sat in a pile to one side, and he resisted the urge to flip them over. The Man's eyes, even rendered in charcoal on paper, bored into his soul.

"My head is swimming with all of these names," he said. "Birth names and married names." He picked up one scrap. "And how did a girl called Naidrie become Nadara?"

"Wait, what did you say?" Ellie said, leaning over his shoulder to peer at the scrap of paper.

"Well, there's a list of the daughters of the Stormbringer, but here it changes. Naidrie to Nadara."

Ellie shook her head. "No, it should be Naidrie to Naidra, and Nadarie to Nadara. Mammy? We found something."

"Naidra," Mammy Berga said, nodding. "It's in my room."

Ellie hurried out of the main room, and Tam looked at Mammy Berga. "I don't understand."

"Ellie and I have been collecting all of this information since the time she was a little girl. We made that list of the daughters of the Stormbringer to help us keep track of what we'd found. But we made a mistake, and skipped from a mother's birth name to her daughter's married name. We've had another piece of the puzzle—Naidra's diary—right under our noses and never realized it till now." She smiled. "Mayhap you can help."

Ellie walked back into the room, her arms wrapped around a small book. "There's something. Naidra had started a list of the names. She calls it a litany. But it's not complete, even for her own time."

"What does it do?" Tam asked.

Ellie grinned. "Assuming it really works? It'll weaken him. Maybe enough that we could banish him."

"But if he goes away, will he still control the rain?"

Mammy Berga shook her head. "I don't think he will. It's worth a try, anyway."

"You'll have to distract him while I recite all of these names," Ellie said, picking up the list, which she now carefully appended with two additional names. "It'll take me a while."

"Won't he try to stop you?" Tam said, a frown creasing his brow. He didn't like the idea of Ellie putting herself in danger.

"Mayhap," she said. "But that doesn't mean it's not worth trying." She took his hand. "Storm's breaking. Let's go out to the orchard and see."

~

46

"So how do we summon him?" Tam asked. He and Ellie stood together in the orchard, her hand in his. His clothes hadn't dried much in front of the fire, but he wanted to face The Man in something other than a bedspread.

"Blood generally works."

"Of course." Tam fished around for his pocket knife and handkerchief. Withdrawing his hand from Ellie's, he turned away from her and sliced open the palm of his left hand. He dribbled the blood on the ground, then wrapped his hand with the handkerchief. "And now?"

"Either he'll come before the blood dries, or he won't."

A rising wind drowned out anything more Ellie might have said. The Man stepped out from behind a tree, and the wind stopped as abruptly as it had begun. He sniffed the air and narrowed his eyes at Tam. "Blood from a young man? What do you think that will accomplish?"

Tam interposed himself between The Man and Ellie. "I've got a proposition for you. Hear me out."

Behind him, Ellie muttered under her breath. "Andie, later Anda, the Bringer of Storms—"

The Man inclined his head to one side, a sly smile spreading across his face. "Oh, by all means. I can only imagine what sort of important proposition a boy in wet clothes has for me."

Tam looked at The Man. "I'm not afraid of you."

The Man laughed. "You should be."

"I want to marry Ellie. I don't want her to be bound to some deal her ancestor made with you. There are plenty of other girls in the village who share some of Lady Anda's blood. My sister, Brina, is one of them. If she's willing to take Ellie's place, will you have her?"

"No."

"Why not?"

"That's not part of the deal. I have honored both deals the way that Lady Anda proposed them. If you wish to alter the deal now, we'd have to start over at the beginning of the negotiations." The Man cast a sidelong glance at Ellie that caused Tam's hackles to rise. "And to be perfectly honest, I'm rather fond of this one. T'will be a shame to lose her for a year."

"But negotiations are an option?" Tam asked.

"Your beloved has broached such a topic previously with me. It's quite simple, really. I never had the opportunity to have a child of my own. I want a son."

Tam stared at The Man for a long while before he spoke again. "That's Ellie's decision, not mine."

"And she has made her choice in the matter." The Man brushed his hands together, as though wiping dirt from them. "Now then. Are you sure you still want her? Knowing all of her family's sordid history?"

"I'm certain."

"Bear in mind that while she is yours, this whole land will see not a drop of rain. Will you be able to live with that knowledge? That your desire causes others to suffer?"

"Not my desire. My love." Tam looked at Ellie. "Our love. Our love will see us through that time, and through the thirteen years when *your* twisted desires keep her from me. And our love—the offspring of our union—ensures the land will remain fertile long after we are gone. We can handle a drought every twenty-some years, I think."

Ellie's voice rose. "Bergie, later Berga, wife of Mik. And Ellie, the Stormbringer of now. Now, Tam, now!"

Tam leapt toward The Man, pocketknife in hand. He thrust the blade into The Man's midsection. It skittered off the fine white suit as though it was armor.

The Man raised his hand and brought it down, open palmed, against the side of Tam's head. Tam felt the impact when a nearby tree knocked the wind out of him. He crumpled to the ground. He reached around blindly for his pocketknife but could not find it.

"Now then, Ellie, were you really thinking about marrying that little worm?"

Tam looked up as Ellie stooped to pick something up from the ground near The Man's feet. His vision blackened, and blood pounded in his ears. It reminded him of the time he had fallen from his horse, and Ellie had come rushing to his aid as he passed out.

Only this time, her voice was not soft and concerned. It was fierce. "Yes, I'm going to marry him, you bastard."

A gasp of pain followed, but it was not Ellie's. Tam forced himself to stay conscious. Though the scene was dim, both from the cloudy night and his wavering vision, light glinted off the handle of his pocketknife between Ellie's delicate fingers. The blade was buried in The Man's stomach. The Man himself was diminishing, and Tam was certain it wasn't just a trick of the blow to the head he'd taken. As he watched, The Man dissolved into nothingness.

"It worked?" he croaked.

"I think so," Ellie said, her voice quiet. "Oh, no, are you alright, Tam?"

"I'll be fine. Just taking a rest while you take care of things."

Ellie smiled briefly, but then looked to the sky, chewing on her lip as she did. "The clouds haven't gone yet."

"Even if they do, it'll be worth it."

"You're right," she said.

Tam rose to his feet and wrapped his arms around her. He murmured her name into her hair—Ella. Ellie was a girl's name. She would go by Ella after they were married.

And then all his thoughts fled from his mind as Ella's lips found his, there in the muddy orchard.mant for 18 years for reasons both practical and best discussed in therapy, but she has been making a respectable living as a consultant, executive coach, and global leadership expert. In 2018, she dyed her hair purple and is starting to turn that all around. This is her first published fiction.

A DARK PLACE

Hunger pangs racked Navar's body, sending spasms through his midsection. He could not remember the last time he had eaten more than a discarded crust of dry bread. Even the food on the ship that had brought him here—moldy and sparse—had been better than nothing.

The sound of carriage wheels rolling across the cobblestones drew his attention. In the three weeks since his arrival, he had seen nothing like the size or grandeur of the gilded carriage that approached. It slowed to a stop in front of him. A gloved hand emerged from the window nearest him and a single finger crooked in Navar's direction. He scrambled to his feet, but before he could move forward, a heavy hand clamped down on his shoulder and turned him around.

"Where'd'ya think you're going, boy?" Brilliant green eyes peered out at Navar from beneath matted gray hair that obscured most of an old man's face.

"The carriage," Navar said. He turned back toward the carriage, disappointed to see that the beckoning hand had already withdrawn into the shadows.

"No, you don't want to get in that carriage. Not if you value your life, you don't."

"Why?"

"You'll thank me for it later," the man replied. "Name's Gratton."

Navar watched the carriage drive slowly away. He sighed, and then introduced himself. "Would you be so kind as to explain why a carriage such as that brings danger?"

"Boy, I've lived in this town my whole life. That carriage has been coming round for the past eight years. And never once has a young man who's gone into the carriage ever returned."

"Perhaps they are given permanent jobs at the estate where they are taken to."

Gratton shrugged. "I s'pose you might think that. But the carriage takes the older men too. At least the ones who don't know better. Brings them back round the next day. And they ain't never seen a young man in that godforsaken place."

"Where does the carriage take them?"

"That big house what overlooks the town." Gratton gestured indistinctly to the west, where a lone hill jutted out of the middle of the forest. "Listen, you're new around here, right? Came in on one of the big boats? Why not just ship back out? You'll do much better for yourself that way."

"I took poorly to shipboard life. Seasickness," Navar said. The heat of embarrassment crossed his cheeks, but he continued on, glad to have someone to talk to. "There are no jobs for learned men where I come from. I spent six years at university, and have nothing to show for it. No trade to speak of. I hoped to find people in search of knowledge and learning here."

Gratton laughed tersely, though the mirth did not reach the old man's eyes. "Well, I'm sure that something'll come your way, a good, smart lad like you."

"Something might have come my way, only you prevented me from reaching it in time. I appreciate your ill-guided attempt to prevent my alleged demise, but unless you have work to offer me, I am afraid I must look elsewhere. Good day, sir."

Navar turned to find a different spot in the town square where he could try to ignore his hunger for a while longer. As he walked away, he heard Gratton mutter, "Suit yourself, then."

~

The next day, with the sun far overhead, Navar looked around for Gratton. The older man was nowhere to be seen. Navar hoped Gratton would not return, but that the carriage would. He suspected that someone with the means to own a carriage of that splendor might have a position for a learned man, and perhaps no need of the typical sort who loitered in the town square. He was not averse to hard work either, if that was requested of him. Anything to provide him a meal would do right now. Navar straightened his shirt over and over again, ran his hands through his hair to smooth it, and stared in the direction the carriage had come from the previous day.

After what felt like hours, the carriage cruised smoothly into the town square. It stopped abruptly, and Navar watched as the hand extended from the carriage window and a single finger beckoned another young man. Navar's heart sank. The other man was scruffy and far more poorly dressed than Navar, seemingly disproving Navar's earnest hope that the owner of the carriage was looking for someone like Navar. The man approached the carriage, and Navar followed him.

The other young man glanced at Navar, then turned back toward the carriage window. "You're wantin' my help?" He addressed whoever was within and ignored Navar.

A long pause followed. Even this close to the carriage, Navar could not see its inhabitants, though he felt as though someone stared at him from its depths. Sweat trickled down his back, and Navar tried to breathe normally to not reveal his fear.

A faint voice emanated from within the carriage. "We will take you both. Two may be better than one."

Navar reached for the carriage door. It swung outward before he placed his hand on the doorknob. He gestured for the other young man to go in. "After you."

"Thank you. Name's Lir."

"A pleasure, Lir. I am Navar."

Navar followed Lir into the carriage. The smell of roasted chicken washed over him. Despite the darkness within the carriage, especially after the brightness of the town square, Navar's apprehension vanished. His sole remaining fear was that if he opened his mouth, he might drool down the front of his shirt. Instead, he strained to locate the source of the aroma.

Two figures sat side by side on one bench in the carriage, dressed in dark, hooded robes. One wore black gloves, while the other, the one who had beckoned through the window, wore white gloves. Navar frowned, unsure why anyone would dress in such a way in warm weather. The figure wearing dark gloves held out a basket, and the scent of chicken intensified.

"You look like you could eat a whole chicken." The voice was deeper than the one that had invited Navar and Lir into the carriage, and much more identifiably masculine. "We didn't figure on two passengers, so you'll have to share."

Navar and Lir both took the basket, placed it on the seat between them, and dived in. By the time they began moving forward, Navar had wolfed down nearly half a drumstick.

~

Navar awoke with a start. He wasn't certain how he had managed to fall asleep with uneaten chicken in hand, but that he still gripped the leg bone was a testament to his earlier hunger. Now he was mostly sated.

As his senses returned, he realized he was still in the carriage, which had stopped moving. Lir was no longer beside him. Navar cursed softly under his breath, fearing that the other young man would be given a position in the household, and that he himself would be returned to the town square. Before he could rise from his seat, a faint rustling sound revealed that he was not alone.

A dark-gloved hand passed through his field of vision and opened the carriage door. "I'll show you to your room."

Navar nodded and stumbled from the carriage. The stable in which he emerged was immense, nearly twice the size of the houses in town. Lanterns hung high on posts throughout the space, illuminating an ornate door set in one of the walls. Navar approached it, curious about the elaborate engraving on what appeared to be something that few would see.

"Please follow me. You must not wander." The dark-gloved man, still covered with hood and robe, moved past Navar soundlessly and opened the door. A shiver slid up Navar's spine. He began to speak, but the other man continued. "Lady Beatrice has asked me to prepare a bath and clean clothes for you. She will meet with you—"

A horrible shriek rent the air, and the servant froze midstep. Navar pressed his hands to his ears, but the sound penetrated through his flesh. The servant grabbed Navar by his shoulders and ushered him down the hallway and into a dark room. As soon as the heavy wooden door closed, the sound diminished. A moment later, it stopped entirely.

"That was Lir, wasn't it?" Navar whispered.

The servant waited before responding. "Lady Beatrice will see you now. We will dispense with the grooming." He returned to the hallway.

Navar paused in the doorway. If the sound had been Lir, then perhaps Gratton had been right about the perils that awaited him here. Perhaps venturing forward was not the wisest choice. Navar looked back down the hall toward the stable, considering heading in that direction rather than following the servant.

But he was not ready to admit Gratton had been right yet. There could be reasons why Lir had screamed. Perhaps the task at hand involved a deformed person, and Lir had been unable to stomach the sight. Navar took a deep breath to settle his resolve, and followed the servant.

The hallways seemed unnaturally quiet, particularly now that the screaming had ended. Navar calculated the turns they made and was shocked by how large the estate must be—easily three or more times larger than his family's substantial home in Near Mezza. They passed no one as they walked, despite the fact that such a place would require a veritable army for a staff. As Navar cleared his throat to ask the servant where everyone was, the servant stopped before a door and knocked softly.

"Enter." The voice beyond the door was husky, but sounded as though it might belong to a woman. The servant gestured to the door, and Navar did as bidden.

Seated inside was a woman dressed entirely in black. Her clothing seemed to pull all the light in the room toward her. Her hair, a wild mass of dirt-colored curls, spilled across her shoulders. In the midst of their tangles, a fierce gaze drew Navar's attention.

"My servants tell me that you declined my invitation yesterday, and yet now you are here. How has this come to pass?"

"I was prevented from entering your carriage yesterday, milady." Navar dropped his gaze as he bowed.

"Prevented? You are a strapping lad. Who could prevent you from going where you would?"

Navar hesitated and looked up at her. The woman held him in her gaze, and it set his nerves on edge, despite how hard he tried to maintain his composure. "I was told that to come here would not be wise."

"Told by whom?"

"Respectfully, milady, I do not wish to divulge who, but—"

"Very well." She squared her shoulders. "Despite what you were told, you are here. And you refuse to tell me the source of your information. Brave and loyal. That makes you just the sort of young man I'm looking for. Come here."

Navar approached her chair, though trepidation slowed his step, and she rose. Her cool hands grasped his, and she whispered a single word. Before Navar could puzzle out what she had said, the entire room vanished into blackness.

The cloying darkness mired Navar as if he had been cast into a vat of tar. Pressure mounted in his chest, convincing him that if he took a breath, he might drown. He tried to move his arms, but the woman's grip remained tight. Muffled sounds ebbed and flowed around him, a confusing cacophony. He thought he heard the bells of the church in the town square. Then came the cries of seagulls, which shifted to the sounds of merchants hawking their wares. He felt dizzy from trying not to breathe. Instinct urged him to run. Then light returned, and the thick air abated.

In place of the elegant parlor furnishings was a Spartan work space with no visible windows or doors. The damp air hung heavy with the musty smell of earth. He could hear nothing other than the pounding of his heart at first. His breath came in ragged gasps as he took in the room, trying to make sense of what had happened. Large jars weighed down shelves lining the walls, each containing something stranger than the one before. Navar spotted brightly colored botanical specimens, a floating hand twice the size of a man's, and a wavering ball of light that reminded him of the tales of the will-o'-the-wisp.

Lady Beatrice cleared her throat and drew Navar's attention from the orb of light. "It occurs to me that we have not been properly introduced," she said, a slight frown creasing her brow, "which is necessary before I go further with my offer. I am Lady Beatrice Hyand, widow of Lord Swayne Hyand. This is ... was, I suppose, his laboratory."

Years of training in appropriate manners prevailed, cutting through Navar's fog of confusion. He found his voice, and managed a stiff bow. "Navar D'Andre, of Near Mezza. Er, my condolences on your loss."

Lady Beatrice waved a hand. "It was quite some time ago. Now then, the reason I mention my late husband has much to do with why I brought you here. That ball of light that you find so fascinating is all that remains of Lord Swayne Hyand."

"H-h-how?" He was staring at the will-o'-the-wisp again, though he could not recall looking away from Lady Beatrice. "How can a person be reduced to a glowing ball of light?"

"There are certain alchemical rituals that are purported to preserve the soul. I can safely say that, with appropriate preparations, these rituals work. My late husband had taken such precautions, and he left an extensive library of notes on how to restore him to a new shell after his untimely demise."

"Shell?"

"Vessel, or host, if you prefer." She shrugged. "The terminology is imprecise because the magic involved has been translated from a long-dead language. There is, of necessity, much approximation involved."

Navar took a slow step backward, but he couldn't keep his gaze from the vessel. "You've kept your husband's soul in a jar, in the hopes of finding the right new body for it?"

"Indeed. Though I have taken it out now and again to attempt the procedure."

Navar's jaw dropped, but he did not respond. His thoughts whirled with the impossibility of what she suggested. Though he had met magicians in Near Mezza, most had been mere charlatans, their tricks easily disproved. Those who practiced true magic were few and far between and dared not dream of what Lady Beatrice claimed was a reality.

"It has not worked, as of yet. But I have taken these failed experiments as opportunities to fine-tune the ritual. I believe I have isolated the final component, and I am certain of success now. Just last week, I successfully restored two souls to new bodies. You met the recipients of those souls in the carriage today."

"The men with the gloves?"

Lady Beatrice nodded.

Navar frowned. "Where did the souls come from?"

"Here and there. Since my husband's passing, I have sought out those who are dying. When you offer someone who is dying the possibility that they might live on, many are most receptive to a few muttered incantations. Not too unlike what the priests offer."

Navar stiffened at her blasphemy, but realized his reaction was foolish. He suspected that the promises of life beyond this one, whether preached or magically applied, were simply a way of keeping the people happy. But he wondered just how far Lady Beatrice's conviction went. "Ah, I see. And where did the previous souls go?"

"When I have been successful, they remain tethered to their body as well, I believe. It seems that in cases where a man has a strong will, the two souls coexist. For those of lesser will, the original soul is suppressed to some extent. In either case, there can be occasional clashes between the personalities. I am still determining the full extent of the effects, of course."

How many other men had stood in this very spot and learned of what this woman believed herself capable of doing? And how many had agreed to the process? *And probably died screaming like Lir.* Navar released a long breath, fearing the answer to his next question. "And now that you've told me this—"

Lady Beatrice gave him a tight smile, and Navar felt another shiver up his spine. Now that he was aware of her intentions, even her smile looked predatory. "I tell you this because the final component seems to be a willingness on the part of the host. When the host has been unconscious or otherwise not given a choice, the transfer has not worked. If you are willing, I am giving you the opportunity to advance my husband's studies. You will be handsomely rewarded, of course." She laid her hand on his arm and lowered her eyes coyly.

Navar used every bit of his willpower not to jerk away from her touch. Lady Beatrice was an attractive woman, and clearly wealthy as well, but the magic she proposed was abhorrent to him. "And if I refuse?"

She turned her back and stepped away, her brief moment of warmness disappearing. "You have heard the rumors. No young men ever leave this place alive."

Navar paused before he spoke again. He was certain Lady Beatrice was fanatical and likely deluded. He also suspected she was not afraid to kill him or at least have him killed. He could not escape from this room, with no doors or windows. Stalling was his only option. "May I have a few days to think on this proposition?"

Lady Beatrice half turned back to him, her gaze darting between the jar containing her former husband's soul and Navar. After what seemed an eternity, she nodded so quickly that he almost missed it.

"I will give you the time you need to make your decision. You will, of course, not be permitted to leave while you consider my offer. You understand, I'm certain."

"Of course, milady."

~

Late that evening, Navar opened the door to his room. One of Lady Beatrice's servants stood watch outside. "Pardon me for seeming so rude, but I have not asked your name."

"Hector," the servant replied. "My brother is Renalt."

Navar opened his mouth to ask another question of Hector, but then shook his head and returned to his room. He wanted to ask how the man found his new existence, but he could not bring himself to hear the response.

Shortly after midnight, he heard shouting outside. Navar's heart began to race. Although he could not make out the words, it sounded like someone arguing with himself. He had not considered what might happen if two souls in a single person were at war with each other, but thought it wise to be prepared to defend himself. Or perhaps he could use this opportunity to escape. He seized a sturdy-looking chair, light enough to heft, but made of thick enough wood that it might have an impact. As quietly as possible, he opened the door.

Hector stood in the same place where he had been earlier. His words were slurred as he shouted, "If she didn't stink of the privy, that is!" Hector then jerked his head to the right, and shouted, "How dare you impugn the dignity of my family name?"

Navar did not hesitate. He raised the chair above his head and brought it down on Hector's upper back. The chair broke apart, the upper portion detaching from the legs and seat.

The other man did not even stagger, though he did stop shouting. He turned toward Navar. "Do you require assistance, sir?"

Navar hoped his first attempt had just been unlucky. He lifted what remained of the chair, preparing for a second swing. Hector's left arm darted out, lightning fast, and caught Navar's right wrist. Pain shot up the length of Navar's arm, rendering his fingers numb in an instant. He tried to wrench his arm free, but Hector's grip was like a vise, only causing the agony to intensify.

"Please release the chair," Hector said.

The remains of the chair clattered to the floor. Navar lashed out with a swift kick and connected with Hector's knee. But again, Hector did not react to the impact.

"Sir, your struggles are futile, at best. My brother and I were chosen for our strength and stamina. We do not wish to hurt you, as the lady does not approve of such methods. But we cannot allow you to leave. Please return to your room and contemplate the offer Lady Beatrice has made. You will find it is the best option."

If that's the best option, then that means there are other options. I'll find them. But he sighed and nodded, and allowed Hector to lead him back into the room. Hector stepped outside and closed the door firmly. Navar rubbed his arm where Hector had grabbed him, determination dulling the pain in his tender flesh.

~

As the days passed, Navar became certain that the soul-transfer process was far more imperfect than Lady Beatrice admitted. Each night, he awoke to the sound of his guard screaming in the hallway. Not willing to make another attempt at slipping out past the lunatic Lady Beatrice had created, Navar only huddled farther under his blankets until it stopped.

By day, he racked his brain for ways to escape, unlikely though it seemed. Every window he had been able to check had been nailed shut, and no doors were left unlocked for longer than it took people to pass through them. His thoughts returned over and over to the bookshelves in the parlor where he had met Lady Beatrice. The laboratory space had been devoid of books, so it seemed that the parlor also served as the library. And where there were books, there lay the possibility of a different approach to escape.

On the afternoon of the fourth day, he opened the door. He glanced at the servant's gloves to identify which brother he addressed. "Renalt, is the lady in the parlor this afternoon?"

Renalt inclined his head slightly before responding. "She is occupied in the laboratory at the moment, but she is available to you if you have made your decision."

"Thank you, but no. I do not require the lady's presence. I would like to read a few books, if I am permitted."

"Of course, sir. Please follow me."

When they reached the parlor, Renalt opened the door for Navar. "I will await you in the hallway. Shall I inform you when it is dinnertime?"

Navar murmured his assent, scanning the bookshelves. He read a handful of titles on the spines and located the section he believed would be most fruitful for his research. As soon as the door closed behind him, he pulled a book from the shelf and leafed through it. He worked his way along the shelves methodically, before he had assembled a small stack of books on magical rituals.

~

When Renalt entered to announce dinner, several hours had passed. Navar stumbled to his feet. Stacks of books surrounded the spot he had occupied on the floor. He picked up a single tome. "Am I permitted to bring a book back to my room?"

Renalt hesitated, but then nodded slowly. "I will send Hector to put away the remainder."

Navar only picked at his dinner as he puzzled over the text, which was written in a language that bore a faint resemblance to Old Draneus. He had identified a passage that made reference to a "dark place." As he paused for a sip of wine, he realized where he had seen some of the words previously. A story in an old religious text he had tried for months to translate while at the university had turned out to be a simple cautionary tale mothers told their children. But enough of the words matched those in this tome that he began to piece together the details of the spell described. He set aside his plate and cup, and ran his finger over the text, excitement mounting.

Home. One must focus on home to arrive there.

~

Less than half an hour later, he stood before Lady Beatrice in the parlor. "I am ready to undergo your procedure."

Lady Beatrice arched one eyebrow and regarded him. Finally, she nodded. "Very well. Come here."

Navar took the lady's hands, certain his sweating palms would reveal his intentions. She gave no indication that she had noticed and spoke the word that would transport them to the laboratory.

The world went dark. Navar tore his hands from Lady Beatrice's and began to run in the opposite direction. At first, the darkness surrounded him, like falling into a muddy bog. His heart raced as the air gained weight and pressed in around him. It was not the drowning sensation he had felt before, but the terror it induced was similar. He thought of his home in Near Mezza, many hundreds of miles away, but the feeling did not change. He struggled, trying to hone his focus.

His mind slipped to the town square, where he had boarded the carriage that led him to this point. He heard the bells of the town church, and tried to run toward them. Without warning, his feet found purchase and he sprinted in that direction.

Navar could not tell how long he ran. His lungs burned and his legs felt like they had been encased in metal. They threatened to stop moving at any moment. The vista had not changed, and he wondered if he had run away from or toward his fate. Despair began to set in, and his exhaustion only compounded the feeling. He could run no farther. He used the last of his strength to throw himself forward.

Navar collapsed in a heap. Dust filled his nostrils and mouth as he gasped for air. The grit clung to his teeth and crept down his throat. He coughed, taking huge, ragged breaths. Slowly, his strength returned enough that he could pull himself upright.

Every bone in his body ached, but he stood and brushed himself off. He looked around and chuckled when he recognized where he was. He stood in the town square.

"Boy? Sailor boy?" From across the square, Gratton waved and began to make his way toward Navar.

Navar smiled. "I made it back from the—" His voice sounded different. He cleared his throat.

"You should look at yourself," Gratton said softly, turning Navar toward a shop window.

Navar barely recognized his reflection. His hair stuck out at odd angles, with large clumps missing, particularly on the top. His face looked wrinkled and worn. He lifted his hands, which had become spotted and swollen at the joints. Returning his gaze to the window, he noticed that only his eyes, brimming with tears, remained recognizable.

A sob escaped Navar's lips, but with it, relief washed over him. He was alive. He had escaped. The state of his body was inconsequential compared with what he had gained.

He turned back to Gratton. "How did you recognize me?" He caught the older man's eyes and identified what he had not put his finger on before. Though Gratton looked sixty or seventy years old, he had the clear eyes of a young man.

Gratton clapped a hand on Navar's shoulder. "Around these parts, you learn to spot the survivors."

"A Dark Place" originally appeared in *Fictionvale* in December 2014. It was reprinted in *Disturbed Digest* in June 2016.

CATCH

Emmeline winced as a floorboard creaked beneath her foot. Her sister Lari still slept, silhouetted in the moonlight. Emmeline hesitated before taking the final steps to the door, plotting the quietest possible route. With breath held, she turned the knob and pulled the door toward her.

The well-oiled hinges cooperated. But faint light from the hearth spilled through the doorway and fell across the bed. Lari turned and coughed raggedly in her sleep. Emmeline closed the door to their room.

Already dressed, she tiptoed around the small living space, picking up her satchel, filled with scraps from the previous day's meals and a water skin. A few dried loaf ends and overripe fruit were a poor lunch, but they were better than sea water. She contemplated whether she was strong enough to haul a bucket of water from the well without using the creaky old pulley system.

Before she made a decision, another door opened. Emmeline spun to face her mother, sleep-rumpled hair framing the latter's face. "Why are you up, Emmeline?"

Emmeline stuffed her satchel and water skin behind her back, then realized her mother had already seen them. "Fishing," she muttered.

Her mother shook her head. "Fishing is no business for a young woman. How many times must I tell you this?"

"Who will take care of us if I don't?"

"We'll get by, Emmeline. We always do."

Emmeline shook her head. "Lari's been sick for a week, Mama. She hides it from you. I sleep in the same bed as her. She's miserable. We were fine before Papa died, but it's harder now. The money you make from taking in washing is enough for us to eat or to buy the medicine she needs. If I don't fish, then either we don't eat or Lari stays sick."

"You can learn another trade. Something respectable," her mother suggested.

"Fishing is what I'm good at. Why should I try to gain talents in things I've proven I'm horrible at? Things that don't even interest me anyway?"

Her mother's voice grew louder. "Emmeline, you're nearly eighteen years old. You'll never find a husband if you don't learn to conduct yourself like a lady. When was the last time any of the village boys came calling? I haven't seen Yov in weeks!"

Emmeline rolled her eyes. "Yov is a spoiled desk clerk. He's never worked a day in his life. Anyway, maybe I don't care if I find a husband."

Her mother frowned. "You wish to join the Order, then?"

"Why can't a woman just live on her own, or with other women? No husband, no Order." Emmeline sighed, exasperated. "Maybe I'll start a colony of fisherwomen."

"That won't work, and you know it. You need a husband. How else will your colony grow?"

"I'm sure there are plenty of other women who would join me. Women who are tired of being told they need a husband to get by." Emmeline paused, not sure she should continue. Her temper won out. "You're doing fine without a husband."

Her mother looked like she had been slapped. Her eyes grew hard. "Oh? I see. Good luck, then. Go start your colony. If you're so committed to fishing, then don't bother coming home."

Emmeline's mouth fell open. Though she and her mother had fought about her fishing before, this was the first time her mother had given her an ultimatum. "You and Lari will starve without me!"

"No, Lari and I can get by without your help." Her mother crossed her arms over her chest. "It's your choice, Emmeline. Go back to bed. Commit to finding another trade, and you're welcome to stay. Otherwise, I won't have you darkening my doorstep again."

A low growl rose from Emmeline's throat. "Fine!" she exclaimed, turning away from her mother and exiting the house. She cranked the winch on the well, not caring if the creaking woke the entire village. Most of the fishermen's wives were already up anyway, preparing breakfasts and lunches for their husbands.

Emmeline's hands shook as she submerged her water skin into the bucket of cold water. Fear crept in, replacing her anger. Where would she sleep if not at home? How would she prepare her dinner? She considered slipping back inside and staying. Only the memory of the look in her mother's eyes stopped her.

Emmeline set her jaw and capped her water skin. She'd find a way to get by, even if it was rough.

~

Fog shrouded the hills surrounding the bay. The sun had barely made an appearance, and a few bright stars still twinkled overhead. Cool air, tinged with the salty fishy smell of the sea, calmed Emmeline's temper. The water lapped against the boats tied to the dock, but otherwise, the world was quiet—even the seagulls slept. She grinned. Perhaps today would be a good day after all.

Emmeline's father's old boat was the smallest of the bunch, tiny enough to be hauled out of the water rather than tied at the dock. Her father had taught her about sailing when she was young, before he fell ill and died, in the years before her mother cared what Emmeline did with her days.

She checked the rudder and tiller, and raised the small sail she had cut down from a discarded larger sail. Doing it all by herself took longer than it would with help, but no crew was willing to take on a fisherwoman. Veteran crews snatched up boys who wanted to fish. Emmeline worked alone.

A splash jarred her from her tasks. She jerked upright and looked around. None of the fishermen had arrived at the docks, but ripples flowed out from behind a small island in the bay. Emmeline sped through her remaining preparations, while keeping one eye on the tiny land mass.

The wind near the shoreline was not strong enough to launch her boat, so she used her oar to push off. She paddled quietly. When she reached the near end of the island, she steered the boat to skim along the back side.

A slender blonde girl clung to one of the trees on the island. She turned at the sound of Emmeline's boat. The look of surprise on her face mirrored that on Emmeline's. The girl lost her grip and flailed as she slid into the water. Emmeline gasped and paddled closer. But the blonde girl was fine. She bobbed in the water, her sea-green eyes wide as she regarded Emmeline.

Emmeline tried not to stare at the scrap of sail canvas the girl wore wrapped around her chest. A castaway might be driven to wear something so unsuited to the water, but the girl looked too healthy to be a castaway. Emmeline also found her gaze lingering over the curve of the girl's breasts at the edge of the canvas, and her cheeks grew warm. She shook her head to clear it and asked, "Are you all right? Why are you half-dressed and in the water?" Emmeline reached out her arm to the other girl to help her into the boat.

The girl stared at Emmeline's arm, following the line of it to Emmeline's face. "You're not a boy. You're a very pretty girl. Why aren't you wearing a dress?"

Emmeline scoffed. "Have you ever tried to wear a dress while fishing?"

The girl cocked her head to one side. "No. It would get in the way." Her face lit up. "Oh, you're fishing! Can I help?"

"Um, sure," Emmeline said. "Take my arm. I'll pull you into the boat."

"I don't fish in boats. But I can show you where there are plenty of fish. Follow me!" The girl pushed away from the shore, swimming on her back. A glimmer of shimmery blue beneath the surface of the water drew Emmeline's attention. Then the girl rolled over and brought her scaly cobalt tail up out of the water, kicking with a huge splash before she dove.

Emmeline's jaw dropped. A mermaid. The villagers said mermaids brought luck to fishermen. She even knew a handful of fishermen who claimed to have seen mermaids or had sex with mermaids, but she never believed them. And now, here she sat dumbly in her boat as a friendly mermaid (who had called her pretty, which lingered in her thoughts) swam away. Her makeshift sail forgotten, Emmeline dipped her oar into the water and paddled as fast as her arms allowed.

~

The mermaid flipped her tail out of the water from time to time, making it easy to follow her. When she resurfaced, kelp strands adorned her hair, and she held up a wriggling fish. "Catch," she said as she tossed the fish to Emmeline. Emmeline's boat teetered as she reached for the fish. She swatted it down with her oar, eliciting peals of laughter from the mermaid.

"What's your name?" Emmeline asked when the laughter and the boat's rocking subsided.

"Aurin. What's yours?"

"Emmeline. It's very nice to meet you, Aurin. But could you slow down just a bit? Paddling is hard work."

"Why don't you use the sail?" Aurin asked. "Do you need me to ensnare a wind serpent?"

"Wind ... serpent?"

"Spirit of the air. They look like serpents. Small serpents, not like the ones in the deep. I can call one."

Emmeline chuckled. "No, no. We don't need to go anywhere. I'm still stuck on the part where you're a mermaid."

"You've never met one of the folk before?"

"I didn't believe the folk existed. I've never seen any of them— sea folk, forest folk, nothing."

"That's because the forest folk are grumpy. They don't like people. Especially not people who belong on the water, like you."

"I belong on the water?" Emmeline smiled. "Would you mind telling my mother that?"

"I'd be happy to! Does she also have a boat?"

"No, no boat. She lives in the village." Emmeline turned and gestured back toward the land. Her spirits dropped when she saw how far away from the shore she had paddled. The return journey would be arduous, if the wind was not with her in the evening.

"If you bring her out here, I can tell her. I can't go to the village." Aurin cast her gaze downward as she spoke.

Emmeline looked down into the water, surprised at how clear it was here. A school of fish passed beneath the boat, and Emmeline reached for her net.

Aurin shrieked, and Emmeline looked up. The mermaid shook her head and held her hands over her mouth. Finally, she moved them and said, "You can't take me back to the village. I can't go on dry land."

"What? Oh, no, I wasn't going to use this on you. I wanted to catch the fish. You brought me out here to fish, remember?" Aurin nodded but still looked shaken. Emmeline dropped the net. "Alright, no net. How will we catch the fish?"

Aurin smiled, though it took a moment for the smile to reach her eyes, which looked pale gray until the mermaid smiled. Emmeline's heart skipped a beat when Aurin spoke. "I'll sing to them, and they'll fill your boat."

Emmeline stared at Aurin, astonished by how reasonable the mermaid made it sound. "If you can do that, why haven't more of you come to help the villagers?"

"Most of us are too afraid. Humans tend to see what we can do and expect it of us all the time."

Emmeline swallowed hard. Her thoughts had drifted to just that idea. If Aurin could sing the fish into her boat, she'd be able to provide more than enough for her family to eat and trade. She hadn't considered whether Aurin would want to do that.

Lost in her thoughts, Emmeline didn't notice that Aurin had continued talking. Aurin had said something about a girl. "What?" Emmeline asked.

"My last girlfriend was speared on the front of a big sailing ship. We tried to rescue her, but the sailors just caught more of us. And then it started a fashion among the sailors with the huge ships. Now they all strap mermaids to the fronts of their ships."

Emmeline's stomach turned. "That's horrible!"

Aurin nodded solemnly. "I haven't seen her in a very long time. I can't imagine how much it hurts."

Something else Aurin had said stuck with Emmeline. "Wait, you said ... girlfriend. What is that?"

"Oh, what do you call them on land? Wife. My wife."

Emmeline blinked several times before she was able to respond again. "You had a wife?"

"Yes." Aurin spun lazily in the water, her tail glistening in the early morning light.

"But you're a girl. How can you have a wife?"

"I made her."

"Made her?" Emmeline sputtered. "What do you mean?"

"Sea folk aren't born like land babies. If we find a person we love, we ask them if they want to join us. Then they become like us."

This was not like the tales of the folk people told while huddled around the hearth in the wintertime. "How?"

"Magic." Aurin laughed. "You really haven't dealt with any of the folk before. It's how it works with us. None of that messy—"

Aurin twined her fingers, pressing the spaces where they met the palms of her hands together. "—mess."

"Oh." Emmeline's heart fluttered as she thought about Aurin's limbs intertwined with her own. "Can it work the other way too? If I loved one of the folk, could I bring them to dry land to be my wife?"

Aurin paled. "I've only heard one story like that. It didn't end well."

"Why not?"

"You give up mortality in order to grow a tail. If you lose your tail, you age and die."

"Wait, did you say give up mortality?"

She nodded. "We're immortal. It wears on you after a while. That's why I spend so much time near the surface. I like seeing the land dwellers, with their life cycle. It's beautiful to me."

"I don't think you'd say that if you had to live it."

"I lived it for a while," Aurin said, a smile spreading across her face. "I was born on land. A kind old man found me when I was sick and brought me into the water. He loved me like my parents had loved me on land."

Emmeline's fight with her mother that morning came back to her, and she winced. "You're lucky, then."

"As long as I don't get caught, yes. That's why it's so horrible when the land dwellers capture us and force us into service. It's forever."

"Isn't love forever too?"

Aurin's face fell. "Forever is a long time. Most of my people get too sad to love forever."

Shouts in the distance drew Emmeline's attention. She looked back toward her village. The fishing fleet had taken to the water. "I should let you hide from the land ... from the villagers. Would you like to sing some fish into my boat?"

Aurin brightened. "I would love to!"

A part of Emmeline heard a different final word. I would love you.

~

Emmeline approached her mother's house, hauling net in hand. The weight of the fish prevented her from moving quickly, but she also dreaded speaking to her mother. She approached the window to the bedroom rather than the front door.

"Lari?" she called out softly.

She heard footsteps behind her and spun. Yov, dressed in his ever pristine shirt and slacks, stopped and stared at her. "That's a lot of fish."

"I had a good catch today."

"Why are you ... what are you doing by the window?"

Emmeline shifted the net over her other shoulder. The rope tore at her hands, but she tried to ignore it. "I don't want to talk about it."

Yov smiled. "Of course. I'd, uh, offer you some help, but ... new clothes. You understand."

Emmeline nodded. A stiff breeze might knock Yov over if it caught him unaware. She doubted he could carry even half her catch. "Was there something you wanted?"

"No, I just saw you, and thought I'd be polite and say hello. I haven't seen you around lately."

Emmeline jerked her head to the side where she carried the fish. "I've been busy."

Yov turned away from Emmeline. "Milady," he murmured as he bowed.

Emmeline's mother came around the corner and stared at Emmeline. Then she turned back to Yov. "So good to see you, Yov! Would you like to come inside and have a cup of tea with us?"

"Thank you, milady, but I'm headed to the evening chapel service. Perhaps another time?"

Her mother smiled. "We would be delighted. Wouldn't we, Emmeline?"

Emmeline hesitated. Her large catch was certainly the reason for her mother's change of heart. She had no way of knowing if it would last, and even if it did, she was becoming increasingly aware she didn't belong here. "I don't know that I'll be here another time."

"Oh, don't be ridiculous, Emmeline. Take those fish inside so we can get them cleaned and ready for market tomorrow."

Emmeline had planned to leave some of the fish for Lari. But she hadn't determined what to do with the rest overnight, until she took them to market, which would take up an entire day. An entire day away from the water. And Aurin, she reminded herself. The choice between sleeping curled up in her boat or stretched out in her bed sealed her decision. Emmeline nodded and brushed past Yov and her mother as she carried the fish inside.

~

Every day for the next month, Aurin met Emmeline behind the island. They spent their days far from land, talking and filling Emmeline's boat with fish. Though she knew the villagers had noticed her increased catches, Emmeline never spoke of Aurin to her mother, Lari, or anyone else in the village.

One morning, Aurin didn't give her usual greeting splash. Emmeline hurried through her preparations and paddled out to the island. Aurin was not there. The sunrise caught a glint of gold, and Emmeline moved her boat closer.

Strands of blonde hair hung from a piece of loose bark. Lower on the tree, an iridescent hand print gleamed. Emmeline placed her hand over it. She pulled her fingers away and caught a faint scent on the breeze. Aurin.

Frantic, Emmeline paddled around the island, calling out the mermaid's name. Finding no sign of her, she headed for the place where they fished. Still nothing. She peered into the deep water. No fish swam there today.

Emmeline took a deep breath, trying to slow her heart. Had she said something the previous day that made Aurin sad? Or was Aurin just playing a prank on her? At any rate, she needed a catch today. Lari had developed a rash on her legs. The cost of the medicine would require several days' catch.

Emmeline hadn't used her large net since the day she met Aurin. The ropes were stiff from hot days baking in the sun. She cast it out half-heartedly, hoping the dreaded device might bring her friend out of hiding.

Her thoughts lingered on Aurin all day. She missed their playful chatter that made the day go more quickly. Though the fishing only took a few minutes of their time these days, Emmeline always stayed out on her boat just as long as the fishing fleet did. Only reluctantly did the two say their goodbyes at the end of each day, even though the time until they would see each other again was never long.

This day stretched out into an eternity. Emmeline alternated between staring at the empty net and scanning the horizon. Once or twice, she thought she caught a glimpse of Aurin's beautiful tail arcing out of the water. Each time, it was only sunlight hitting the waves at an unusual angle.

By the time she sailed back to shore, Emmeline's stomach was knotted with worry. She had hauled in only half the fish she had caught in the days before Aurin; her mother would be upset. Emmeline wasn't worried about her mother's disappointment, even if it led to another argument. She was worried about Aurin.

She usually ignored the fishermen as they hauled in the fleet and their catch. They left the lone fisherwoman to her business, and she left them to theirs. But faint laughter from some of them as she picked up her meager catch made her face burn red, and tears threatened to spill from her eyes. She took a deep breath and looked up to see if she could spot one of her neighbors.

"Ban," she called out, beckoning the boy over.

"What do you want?"

"Could you take these to my mother? Tell her I've gone out for more."

"Are you crazy? You're going out to fish at night?"

"I just ... This isn't enough. I need more."

"Well, alright. But you're gonna miss out. Yov's gone mad. He's been drawing water from the well all day long."

Emmeline frowned. "Why?"

"No one knows. He hasn't let anyone in his house all day either. Vic thinks he's cleaning before he asks someone to marry him, but no one knows who he's courting."

Emmeline's stomach turned. There had been a time when she suspected Yov would ask for her hand. And of course her mother would give it, not waiting to hear Emmeline's opinion. Was Yov cleaning house before he asked her to be his wife? Emmeline couldn't bear that thought. If she could convince him he didn't want her, it might be the only way out of marrying him. "Never mind. I'll take these home myself."

Ban smirked. "Suit yourself."

Emmeline took a different route home—one that took her past Yov's house. A group of villagers lingered on the street nearby, talking in hushed tones. Emmeline looked at the ground outside Yov's house. When her mother cleaned their house, the stones outside glistened with the remnants of the cleaning water. Yov's yard was dry, save for a few splashes near the door. Sloshing noises came from inside the house.

Most of the crowd looked away from Emmeline, but she spotted her sister. "What's happened?" she whispered, crouching down to Lari's eye level.

"Someone said they saw him with a girl early this morning. I thought it could be you. But then he started carrying buckets of water. Everyone's afraid. Are you here to talk to him?"

Emmeline kissed Lari on the forehead. "Don't worry, I'll be careful." She rose and knocked on Yov's door. When no one answered, she pushed on the door, which swung open. Emmeline paused. The house was dark inside, the shutters drawn. She glanced back at the gathered crowd. Everyone except Lari pointedly ignored her inquiring gaze. She stepped inside cautiously.

In the center of the room sat a large wooden trough, twice as big as the ones used to water livestock. It was nearly full, though the floor around it was covered in water. Emmeline peered into the water. A splash made her jump back a foot, but as soon as she recognized the source of the splash, she moved forward again. It took little light for Emmeline to identify the blue of Aurin's tail. She reached down and found Aurin's hand.

Aurin surfaced quickly. Her small canvas shirt was stuffed into her mouth as a gag, and her hands were bound in front of her. Although her face was red and blotchy, her eyes lit up, shifting from gray to green as soon as they landed on Emmeline's face. Emmeline fumbled at the knots on the sodden fabric while Aurin slung her bound hands over Emmeline's head and around her neck. It took all of Emmeline's willpower to remain focused on the task at hand with Aurin's naked breasts pressed against her.

As soon as her mouth was free, Aurin wailed, "You must get me back to the sea. This water is horrible."

Emmeline looked at the trough. Filled with water, it was impossible for her to move. "How long can you survive out of water?" she asked.

"Forever, I suppose," Aurin replied. "But I cried the whole time that boy was carrying me here. It hurt a lot."

Emmeline nodded and began to work on the rope binding Aurin's hands together. "I'll carry you straight back to the sea. We'll have to trust it will work. Do you trust me?"

"With all my heart," Aurin said.

Emmeline slipped her hands under Aurin's arms and lifted her a little more out of the water, enough so their faces were at the same level. "I love you, Aurin. Once I get you out of here, I want you to take me with you and make me your wife. We'll go far away from here."

Aurin smiled. "I feel the same way, but if I tell you that now, we'll both be stuck in this horrible water, suffering. That's the magic. Those three words."

Light spilled across the trough, and Emmeline let go of Aurin. She spun to face the door. Yov pulled the door shut behind him and approached Emmeline. He shook his head, a wry smile on his face. "So, you came for her."

Emmeline shot a look at Aurin. "Yes. How did you know about her?"

"Fishermen gossip just as much as women do." Yov shrugged. "You row your boat out much farther than the rest of the fleet, but not far enough to be out of their sight."

"So you kidnapped her? Why?"

"She's an abomination. It's not natural. I've called for the priest. He will burn the impurity from her."

Emmeline moved away from the trough, putting herself between Yov and the door. "Ban was right. You've gone completely mad."

"Mad? No. Not mad. Blessed. You, on the other hand, have gone mad. But I have plans to fix you as well. Your mother's given me permission to marry you, which in this case will have to do. I couldn't ask your father."

Emmeline clenched her fists. "First mistake, you think my mother has any control over me. Second mistake, you brought up my father. Actually, let's back up a step. Your real first mistake was kidnapping my ... wife."

"Wife?" Yov exclaimed. "How can you marry a monster? I'll have the priest marry us just as soon as your 'wife' here is purified."

"No." Emmeline stepped backward and fumbled for the bar for Yov's front door. She hefted it behind her back, but she couldn't slide it home without turning around. The last thing she needed was for Yov to get reinforcements. But turning her back on a madman seemed an equally risky proposition.

76

The old priest from her childhood was several years gone, taken in the same epidemic that took her father. She hadn't gone to church since the new priest arrived in town, but he didn't look friendly. And he seemed to be the source of Yov's obsession with calling Aurin a monster. She turned and barred the door.

When she turned back to face Yov, he had picked up one of the fish she had dropped on the floor. Holding it by the tail, he swung it toward her face. She grabbed it instinctively, barely feeling the scrape of its scales across her calloused hand, and pulled it from his grasp.

"You just attacked me with a fish?" she asked, tossing the fish aside. Before he responded, Emmeline lunged at him. Yov danced out of her reach, putting the trough between them. Emmeline looked around for something to throw at him, settling on a piece of crockery. Aurin clung to the side of the trough and watched the pot sail across the room, which Yov easily sidestepped.

Fists pounded on the door. "Yov?" Emmeline didn't recognize the voice. Yov glanced toward the door, but Emmeline remained between him and it.

"Look, I'm not letting your priest in here. And I won't leave without her. We can stand here and stare at each other all night if you'd like—"

Yov rushed her. Emmeline lunged at him, grappling his torso and pinning his arms to his sides.

"Well, if I had known you would grab me like this, perhaps I would have just let you." He smirked, his face inches from hers.

"Emmeline, throw him in the water!" Aurin cried out.

It took Emmeline a moment to realize what Aurin was asking her to do. But when it dawned on her, she grinned. "Ready? Catch!" She planted her feet and rotated the upper half of her body. Her arms had grown strong in the month of chasing Aurin, and Yov could not stop her from throwing him.

Aurin rose up out of the trough and caught Yov. She clenched her arms around his torso and pulled him down into the water. Yov flailed his legs. Water splashed outside of the tub. Something heavy slammed against the door. Emmeline spared a glance at it. The bar still held. She rushed to the side of the tub and grabbed for Yov's legs.

Aurin surfaced. "Hold down his chest!"

Emmeline did as instructed, dodging Yov's increasingly feeble kicks. A thought gave her pause. "Aurin, we're not going to kill him, are we?"

"Well, mermaids are known for drowning men," Aurin admitted. "Just hold him a bit longer, and he should pass out."

Yov continued to thrash around, and Emmeline coughed as she sucked down water. She stumbled back a step. Yov's head rose out of the water. Still struggling for breath, Emmeline shoved Yov's chest downward, submerging his head again. Finally, he stopped moving. Aurin hauled him out of the water and dropped him on the floor of his cottage.

Emmeline rolled him onto his side and clapped him on his back twice. Yov did not respond. She looked up at Aurin. "He needs the medicine woman."

Aurin leaned forward and brushed her hand across Yov's lips. He coughed and sputtered, water pouring from his mouth and nose. "We also have been known to save some men from drowning. Even if they don't deserve it."

Emmeline stared at Aurin, while Yov lay limp on the floor, still clearing the water from his lungs. "Remind me to never make you unhappy."

"I don't think you can, you beautiful girl!"

~

Carrying Aurin in a sling with enough seawater to keep her tail covered was difficult. Emmeline was too happy to care. The villagers watched in silence. Few of them had ever seen one of the folk.

Lari stood at the door to their house, mouth agape. "Is she a mermaid?"

Emmeline smiled at her sister. "Yes. Aurin, this is my little sister Lari. Lari, this is Aurin. Where's Mama?"

Lari pointed at the house. "In there."

Emmeline rolled her eyes. "Mama? Please come out. I can't fit through the door carrying my wife."

"Your what?" Emmeline's mother scurried into the doorway.

"My wife. We're going down to the bay after this. Aurin is going to make me a mermaid. I won't be back after tonight."

"How will we ... what will we do without you?"

"You'll get by. Aurin and I have agreed that we'll fill my old boat with fish every morning until Lari is old enough to become a fisherwoman. Or to take up any trade." She looked her mother in the eyes. "Let her do what she wants. Keep her close but let her free too." She swallowed hard. "Please."

Her mother's eyes filled with tears. Emmeline's vision blurred as her own eyes grew moist. Lari, the only member of the family who seemed unaffected by Emmeline's plea, moved to their mother's side to hug her. "We'll be fine, Emmeline. Just bring less fish until my arms get stronger."

"We will," Emmeline agreed. "I love you both. But it's time for me to have a family of my own." She looked at Aurin. "It's time."

Aurin loosed one of her arms to wave to Lari and Emmeline's mother, then resumed her previous position. Emmeline turned and walked toward the shore.

When they reached the shore, Emmeline lowered Aurin back into the water. The mermaid stretched, her tail rippling in the setting sun. "Swim with me," she said.

Emmeline pulled off her boots and then slipped into the water to finish undressing. "I hope this works."

"It will." Aurin wrapped her arms around Emmeline's neck. "I love you."

ABOUT THE AUTHOR

Dawn Vogel's academic background is in history, so it's not surprising that much of her fiction is set in earlier times. By day, she edits reports for historians and archaeologists. In her alleged spare time, she runs a craft business, co-edits *Mad Scientist Journal*, and tries to find time for writing. She is a member of Broad Universe, SFWA, and Codex Writers. Her steampunk series, *Brass and Glass*, is being published by Razorgirl Press. She lives in Seattle with her husband, author Jeremy Zimmerman, and their herd of cats. Visit her at historythatneverwas.com.

ABOUT THE ARTIST

Leigh's professional title is "illustrator," but that's just a nice word for "monster-maker," in this case. More information about them can be found at http://leighlegler.carbonmade.com/.

www.ingramcontent.com/pod-product-compliance
Lightning Source LLC
Chambersburg PA
CBHW060953120626
46557CB00003B/1150